DOCTOR'S REQUEST

Mandy was suddenly faced with a task that had little to do with nursing, but it was the only way to keep a certain doctor's attention. Complications followed when she discovered that Leigh's heart was set on the attractive Sister who ran the ward Mandy worked on. When the mystery deepened, Mandy had to endure disappointment and anguish, but the doctor was not as disinterested as he appeared to be.

MARJORIE CURTIS

DOCTOR'S REQUEST

Complete and Unabridged

LINFORD
Leicester

First published in Great Britain in 1984 by
Robert Hale Limited
London

First Linford Edition
published 1996
by arrangement with
Robert Hale Limited
London

British Library CIP Data

Curtis, Marjorie
    Doctor's request.—Large print ed.—
Linford romance library
1. English fiction—20th century
I. Title
823.9'14 [F]

ISBN 0–7089–7902–5

Published by
F. A. Thorpe (Publishing) Ltd.
Anstey, Leicestershire

Set by Words & Graphics Ltd.
Anstey, Leicestershire
Printed and bound in Great Britain by
T. J. Press (Padstow) Ltd., Padstow, Cornwall

This book is printed on acid-free paper

1

IT was at Sister North's farewell party that Mandy first met Leigh Guthrie. And it was an occasion that she never forgot.

Not that Dr Guthrie took much notice of her! Their eyes met fleetingly when they were introduced but he turned away almost immediately to speak to someone else. The doctor was a friend of Sister's fiancé and made it obvious that he was not much concerned, with the bevy of young nurses who were twittering away excitedly.

Even so, Mandy was conscious of an intense awareness of him. So much so that she was rather bemused for the rest of the evening in spite of having more than her fair share of attention from the staff she worked with.

"What's the matter with you tonight,

green eyes?" Tony Southwood whispered in her ear as he passed to refill his glass.

She shook her red-gold head and laughed. "Nothing! Why? Do I look peculiar?"

"Hardly! Bewitching, more like! Who is the lucky fellow?" he teased.

Mandy pulled a face at him. He grinned, shrugged his shoulders and moved on. She took it all in good part for she was used to him. But inwardly she did warn herself to be careful, to hide that inner excitement that was threatening to engulf her.

Yet if Mandy had been an invisible witness to a conversation taking place later that evening, she might have felt apprehensive not exhilarated.

Sister North had drawn Dr Guthrie aside so that she could speak to him in private. He made no objection because he was anxious to discuss something important with her.

"Mark and I will have to leave soon," she told him, raising her voice in order to be heard above the din. "I want to apologise for letting you down with the colonials."

Leigh smiled wryly. "You don't look sorry. I bet you are glad that you have a valid excuse. That's the truth, confess now, Kathryn!"

"Perhaps. But you can't expect me to say so." Her blue eyes darkened as she gazed reflectively at her guests.

Leigh frowned at her lack of interest. "You have thrown me to the lions!" he grumbled. "What am I to do? I can't let old Perkins down. He's just offered me Reggie's job."

Kathryn smiled. "It sounds like a spot of blackmail to me!" she said lightly.

"I suppose it's all part of the day's work," Leigh said gloomily. "You might look and sound more sympathetic! Can't you suggest something I can do?"

"Mandy Greenwood might be willing to help you out," Kathryn replied uncertainly.

"Who is she? Do I know her?" Leigh replied quickly.

Kathryn laughed. "Don't tell me you didn't notice her! She's the pretty redhead. I did introduce you."

"I didn't take much notice." Leigh's eyes sought Mandy's slender figure. He sighed and gave Sister North a reproachful look. "You can't be serious! She's much too young. I need someone more mature and sensible."

"I can't see why! Don't let Mandy's looks fool you. She's a very efficient little lady. You ought to consider yourself lucky if she decides to help you. She's more seriously minded than other young women of her age."

"How old is she?" Leigh looked unconvinced.

"Twenty-three, I think. She's been nursing for five years. She does well in exams."

That's of no consequence to me!" Leigh said irritably. "Can't you recommend anyone else?"

"Not at such short notice!" Kathryn smiled wickedly. "There's Sister Lucas, of course. She wouldn't refuse you."

"No, thanks!" Leigh said hastily. "If you can think of a suitable person, let me know before you go."

"There's not enough time! This is farewell. I won't be seeing you again for some time. Mark and I have a train to catch."

Leigh was suddenly contrite. He bent down and kissed her cheek.

"Don't give my problems another thought!" he told her. "It was selfish of me to mention them. I hope the change goes well. Am I going to be asked to the wedding?"

"I expect so," Kathryn said vaguely. She was beginning to feel tired and was anxious to take her leave of the others.

The party broke up soon after the taxi arrived to take Sister North and her fiancé to the station. Leigh stayed on longer than he had intended. He felt curious about the girl Sister had recommended and was annoyed with himself for not paying more attention when he was introduced to her.

He noticed that she appeared to be popular with the men in her group and outshone the other girls. Also she was not behaving so atrociously as one or two of the younger nurses whom he vaguely recognised. They had been drinking too much and were unconscious of the noise and ill-mannered shouting that was spoiling the fun for the other guests.

Perhaps Kathryn is right, Leigh mused. She certainly seems more mature than the rest of her bunch. I wouldn't have picked any of them. She's very attractive but looks scarcely matter. An older woman would be easier to deal with.

I won't decide yet, he told himself rather tiredly as he made his way out. Kathryn wasn't over enthusiastic about helping and I doubt if anyone else will be inclined to assist me; least of all a youngster with her own concerns to see to. I will have to consider it carefully before I make the first move.

★ ★ ★

Back on the ward the next morning, Mandy's bemused feeling had vanished. She had pulled herself together and was her normal level-headed self.

Sister's drinks must have been more potent than I realised, she told herself good-humouredly. I felt like a princess at a ball only it wasn't as grand as that . . . just a social affair to wish Sister all the good things in life. Mark seemed just the right fiancé for her. I hope they enjoy working together in Yorkshire. She is going to be sorely missed by the nurses she helped to train.

Mandy sighed reflectively as she joined her friend, Audrey to get their instructions from Staff Nurse. There were some exciting people there last night, she thought. I wish I had had the chance to find out more about them.

"Did you two enjoy yourselves last night?" Moira inquired good-naturedly.

"Yes. It was a pity you weren't able to come," Audrey replied.

"Sister and I had a little celebration earlier in the week," Staff Nurse told them. "There's a lot to do this morning, so forget the chit-chat. I've made a list . . . thought that might be easier for you. I wasn't sure how clear your heads would be this morning." Mandy laughed. "It wasn't that kind of a party!"

"Just as well!" Staff retorted. "Get going, sluice-room first!"

The two nurses groaned audibly as they scurried off. Staff Nurse had an amused smile on her lips. There was nothing like hard work for restoring a nurse to her senses!

In spite of being fully occupied that morning, Mandy found it increasingly difficult to concentrate. Several times her friend had to remind her to pay

8

attention to what she was doing.

"You are in a daze today!" Audrey ejaculated. "Don't you feel well?"

"I'm fine." Mandy smiled ruefully. "I keep thinking of last evening."

Audrey raised her eyebrows in exasperation. Taking an armful of bed linen from the trolley she thrust it at Mandy.

"Next bed and don't drop it!" she warned her. "The party wasn't that good!" she added bluntly as they swiftly sorted out the covers.

"It was marvellous!" Mandy protested.

"Perhaps it was for you." Audrey gave her a shrewd look. "You did seem very excited. Even Tony remarked that you were in high spirits."

Mandy frowned. "He would put it like that! I didn't have much to drink. I was more interested in Dr Guthrie. He looked so handsome."

"So that's it!" Audrey laughed as she threw a corner of the top blanket for her to catch. "You are smitten at last!"

"Don't be silly!" Mandy retorted

quickly. "We only said two words to each other."

"A look will suffice." Audrey stopped what she was doing and stared at her friend anxiously. "I do hope you aren't serious. He's got a reputation for being unreliable."

"How do you know that?" Mandy asked doubtfully.

"He used to work here. Most of the nurses were wary of him after Sister Mortimer left. She was nuts about him."

"I've not heard her mentioned."

"It was before you came here. You haven't been at St Adrian's as long as I have."

"I trained at St Mark's first. Do tell me what happened!"

"I don't really know. Sister Mortimer used to go about with Dr Guthrie. Then one day we heard she had left. There was a lot of talk. Dr Guthrie came out of it badly. He left also, not long after, so, the mystery was never cleared up."

10

"I expect they agreed to part," Mandy said carelessly.

"I bet she didn't," Audrey said. "She never bothered to hide her feelings. As I said before she doted on him."

"Perhaps it's best to give doctors a wide berth," Mandy said dejectedly. "You can't trust many of them."

"How right you are! I expect they say the same about the nurses." Audrey leaned across the bed and exclaimed warningly, "Look out! Staff is sailing towards us. She doesn't seem all that pleased."

"Oh dear! I suppose we have been a long time."

"What have you two been doing?" Staff demanded in a fierce voice. "No, I shouldn't have asked that! It's pretty obvious. If you two can't work without all this chattering I will have to separate you . . . move one of you to another ward!"

Mandy and Audrey exchanged glances of horror. Both sighed with relief when Staff Nurse moved away after a final reminder to get on with their tasks.

"She couldn't do that, could she?" muttered Mandy.

"She could suggest to Sister that we be moved," Audrey said. "That was a close one and no mistake. She was mad with us!"

The two nurses hurriedly smoothed the coverlet and moved on to the next bed to be made up. Both felt slightly shaken at the thought of being parted.

"I've seen her standing talking for ages to her pet consultant!" Mandy grumbled in defiance.

"She is one of the seniors." Audrey chuckled. "Never mind, cheer up! She could have been much nastier. We have taken our time. We were supposed to see to the elevenses. Rosemary has nearly finished with them."

"She is a dear. She never moans."

"She's not been here long enough!" Audrey said lightly. "Wait 'til she does a spell on nights!"

"Yes. I'm afraid it will test her

endurance. I used to dread it."

"It frightened me, too, at first," Audrey agreed.

Both girls were working full out now. Staff Nurse passed by and nodded her head approvingly.

"Eight at night until eight the next morning is a long shift," Mandy remarked. "There was only one other nurse the first time I changed over. I was terrified something might happen that we couldn't cope with."

"We won't have to do that for a while," Audrey said with a sigh of satisfaction.

"Don't be too sure! We have to accept the current situation. Shortage of staff affects us all. Our burden becomes heavier not lighter."

"That's why Sister and Staff don't come down too heavily when we stray from the straight and narrow. They are both fairly reasonable. I have worked under far worse seniors."

"We may be seniors ourselves soon," Mandy said. "Our next lot of exams will decide that."

"I'm not at all confident," Audrey told her gloomily. "I'm so inattentive in the lecture room. I keep nodding off."

Mandy smiled. "You aren't the only one!"

★ ★ ★

A week later found both girls having lunch together. It was unusual because Staff Nurse preferred one of them to remain on the ward. But that afternoon Mandy was due in the children's unit. She would not be far away because it was attached to the women's medical ward. So it was a pleasant treat for them to be able to share their midday meal. Mandy took the opportunity to ply her friend with the questions that had been nagging at her for days.

"Tell me about Sister Mortimer," she begged after they had selected their food at the lunch counter.

Audrey's brown eyes softened with indulgent amusement. "Are you still thinking about Dr Guthrie?"

"I'm just interested," Mandy replied offhandedly.

"Mm . . . What do you want to know?"

"What she looked like, how old she was . . . you know!" Mandy exclaimed impatiently.

"She was, at a guess, about twenty-eight," Audrey said carelessly. "Her hair was dark. Summing up I would say she had a good figure and was quite attractive."

"That figures," Mandy said with a faint frown. "Dr Guthrie gave me the impression that he preferred a woman to have good looks."

"I agree. I've seen him with other girls. They were all fairly outstanding."

"You needn't rub it in!" Mandy sighed. "Anyway I needn't worry on that score. I don't suppose I shall see him again to speak to intimately. Isn't it maddening? You meet someone to whom you are attracted and you can do nothing about it! A man would get in touch somehow."

"Some girls would do the same." Audrey grinned. "Not you, I guess!"

Mandy shook her head. "I wouldn't dare! He would consider it presumptuous. I'm pretty sure of that."

"Some men might be flattered but it's my belief also that he's more orthodox. He's not a man to be treated lightly. On the other hand if he was drawn to you he might be pleased if you made the first move."

Mandy chuckled. "That's not likely! He scarcely noticed me."

"I know the feeling! It hurts. But it's usually because we all look alike in uniform."

Mandy frowned. "I was in my best party dress!"

Audrey nodded her brown head solemnly. "That does make it worse."

"You are a lot of help! All I need is a little encouragement."

Audrey was silent for a few moments. Suddenly she seemed extremely serious.

"I don't want to encourage you. It's

my opinion that you ought to let well alone. Forget him! You will only get hurt. Sister Mortimer couldn't have been a nicer person. Yet look what happened to her. And there must have been other poor unfortunates."

Mandy smiled at her friend's long face. "You make him sound dreadful! I'm not going to cast myself at his feet! I might not like him if the chance arose to know him better."

"That's quite likely! At the moment you are seeing him through rose-coloured glasses. Try to view him unemotionally."

"How can I be emotional when I don't even know him! Your advice is about as good as nothing!" Mandy exclaimed.

"Thanks very much! I shall remember that next time you want succour and comfort."

"I feel very unsettled."

Audrey smiled. "That's exam fever. You will feel better when they are finished." She hurriedly finished her

17

orange juice then added, "I must go. You needn't come. You aren't due yet in the children's ward. Give my love to Violet!"

Mandy smiled to herself after her friend had gone. Audrey never forgot to mention Violet. She was a crippled eight-year-old, who had to attend hospital at intervals. All the staff were fond of her. She was a small, dainty child in spite of her disfigurement.

When Mandy first saw Violet with the sheet pulled up close to her large brown eyes, she was drawn to the child's bedside in spite of her own preoccupation with her duties. The eyes had regarded her so wistfully beneath the mop of dark curly hair. When the elfin face emerged from beneath the covers, Mandy could see the semi-transparent skin of the habitual invalid.

She looks much too white, Mandy thought, her heart twisted with pity. She felt compelled to stop and speak to the child if only for a few minutes.

But Mandy soon discovered that her compassion and pity was a wasted effort as far as Violet was concerned. The child did not feel sorry for herself and did not expect anyone else to feel that way either. She had more courage and confidence than many adults. She was thoughtful and good-tempered which was amazing if one thought of what she had to endure. No one could refer to her as dull. Her sense of humour was catching and any ward with Violet in it was blessed indeed.

The little girl was the first patient that Mandy looked for after she had reported herself to Sister Morris. Mavis, a second year nurse, noticed Mandy standing by the child's empty bed and stopped to explain.

"Violet is in Theatre. She's having another operation," she said.

"Oh, not again!" Mandy looked upset. "That poor child! When will it end?"

"Mr Duffy says it may be the last

one. He has plenty of optimism. I will say that for him."

"I hope he is right," Mandy replied doubtfully. "When is she due back?"

"Any time now," Mavis told her. "She went along there at ten o'clock."

"As long ago as that!" Mandy sounded worried. "It's after two o'clock now."

"They may be keeping her there until she comes round. They are so careful with the little ones."

"Yes, I know. Theatre Sister is wonderful and really makes a fuss of the children. I enjoyed working with her so much."

"Can you give me a hand with the dressings?" Mavis asked as she returned to the trolley she had been pushing. "There aren't many but I want to get them finished with before Mr Duffy comes in. He comes to see his patients every day that he is here. It's usually late afternoon after he's finished in Theatre."

Mandy had always enjoyed helping

out in the children's section although she had never been assigned there permanently. Anxious parents of the children were allowed to visit at odd hours and the very fact that one was liable to come across a strange face, someone not connected with the hospital, made the ward feel less clinical, more homely.

It was fine for the children and parents but extremely trying for Sister who had to sustain a high standard of hygiene and efficiency. As if clutching at a lifeline, she pounced on Mandy who happened to be working nearby. She was used to Sister's swiftness in giving orders and listened very carefully knowing full well that they wouldn't be repeated.

"Go over and chat to Michael's mother for five minutes. Then persuade her to go home. She's been at his bedside for nearly an hour and is upsetting both herself and the child. He ought to be sleeping! Some parents just don't use their common sense!

After you have done that, report back to me."

Mandy scarcely had time to say, "Yes Sister," before the woman was off again. Glancing back over her shoulder, Mandy saw her chiding two of the juniors who had been making too much noise.

Sister has her work cut out, Mandy thought, smiling to herself as she walked towards Michael's bed. The small boy looked at her dully. There were dark smudges beneath his eyes. He could hardly keep them open. His mother was urging him to read the book she had brought in for him. She was looking distressed at her son's lack of co-operation.

"He's not trying," she complained to Mandy who had taken in the small scene with some concern. "He ought to do some homework. He will be so behind when he returns to school."

Mandy smiled at the child then turned her attention to the mother. She had the same look of frustration that

Mandy had seen on many occasions. The son's fair hair and blue eyes were very much like the mother's.

"Michael is intelligent. But allowing him to worry about his place in school won't help his progress here. You want him to be strong enough to come home, don't you?" Mandy's voice was kind and sympathetic as she went on, "He has had such a brave struggle to regain his strength. He tires easily. Don't expect too much of him."

The woman gazed at her doubtfully. "You think I'm pushing him too hard?"

"Just a little. It's natural. Obviously you want him to do well. But his health does come first."

"Yes, of course!" Michael's mother bit her lips nervously. "It's his father, you see. He's so clever himself. He expects Michael to be the same and blames me if he falls behind." She sighed unhappily. "It's difficult to know what to do for the best. I was trying to save him from future harassment."

Mandy gazed at her thoughtfully.

She could see that the woman had real problems. It was not just thoughtlessness as Sister had implied.

"Give him a few days to rest then try again," Mandy said gently. "He will respond more readily if he feels well."

The woman nodded. "You are right. I know that. I wasn't being sensible. I do hope I haven't set him back."

"Leave him now so that he can rest. Try not to be anxious. I'm sure he was pleased to see you. He is in good hands here."

"Yes. Sister Morris has been so encouraging."

Mandy did not have enough authority to discuss a patient's condition. She spoke of other things and gradually drew the woman towards the exit. It had taken longer than five minutes. However she felt gratified when she returned to Michael's bedside to find him fast asleep.

Sister looked pleased when Mandy reported back to her. "Good work. Nurse. You saved me at least thirty minutes. It would have taken me longer to explain. I feel sorry for the woman but I do have other patients to consider. Everyone has problems. I do wish they wouldn't unload them on my shoulders."

"Perhaps a social worker could help," Mandy suggested.

Sister shook her head. "It's best left alone. It's a minor domestic problem. Michael's parents will have to sort it out for themselves. There are many children with over zealous parents."

"His mother gave me the impression that she was scared of upsetting her husband," Mandy said.

"I don't think Michael is in too much danger. His father seemed reasonable enough when I spoke to him." She smiled indulgently at Mandy. "You can't make it your concern. There's not enough time to agonise over every patient. Go and help Nurse Brady with the teas."

If you worked on Sister Morris' ward you had to get used to abrupt dismissals. All the time she had been talking to Mandy, Sister's eyes had been scanning the ward; her mind already projected into concerns that would need her consideration. It gave the listener an uncanny sense of not being there.

Nurses who were with her daily became adroit at picking out the points that most mattered and closing their minds to unimportant issues. It was impossible to take all the instructions in. Orders were never repeated and a newcomer might find herself left stranded and bewildered for at times it was like being under rapid fire.

After the tea trolleys had been wheeled away, Mandy went to the kitchen to check up on the student nurse, suspecting that she would have neglected to sterilise the milk pan. Sure enough, it was standing there unwashed near the sink.

None of them stop to clean milk saucepans, she thought resignedly as she hastened to clean and sterilise it. After that she lingered there not minding having to wash the odd dish of the patients who had to diet. It gave her a chance to dream . . . a habit she ought to have broken long ago. But anticipating a vacation was almost as exciting as actually experiencing it.

Her thoughts were shattered by the noisy entry of a nurse.

"Sister wants you on the ward!" she said cockily. "What have you been up to, Greenwood? She looks pretty grim."

Her mind swiftly cleared of vain fancies, Mandy braced herself for almost anything. But it was too much for her to push through the swing doors immediately, especially as the doors had not been closed tightly.

Through the aperture she was able to see Sister Morris and a tall man she was talking to. He looked vaguely familiar although she could only see the back of him.

Realising that to delay any longer would bring Sister's wrath upon her head, Mandy pushed wide the doors and began to walk quickly towards the pair. When the man turned his head and glanced back at her she was so astonished that she almost stumbled. She righted herself swiftly and bit her lips to prevent the gasp of surprise from being heard.

But she had no such control over her lovely green eyes. They widened considerably as she took in the grave countenance of Dr Guthrie.

2

SISTER was eyeing Mandy critically. "Your uniform is wet! What have you been doing, Greenwood?" she asked sternly.

"I was cleaning up in the kitchen." Mandy felt awkward and apprehensive with Dr Guthrie's eyes upon her.

"You could have left that for the ward maid," Sister told her crisply. "Dr Guthrie wants to have a word with you." She glanced briefly at the doctor. "I have much to do so if you would excuse me?"

"Certainly, Sister!" Leigh Guthrie nodded his dark head. "Thanks for the favour. I won't forget."

Mandy was becoming more and more perplexed. Doubt clouded her long-lashed eyes, kept lowered because she felt too embarrassed to stare at him. What could he want to speak to her about?

Leigh was about as unsure of himself as the nurse was. But when Sister had hurried away he attempted a friendly smile hoping to put the girl at her ease.

"It's rather public here. Shall we move into the corridor?" he inquired.

Away from the ward Mandy felt even more awkward. She moved close to the wall and put her hands behind her back so that she had something firm to contact.

"You look extremely puzzled and I'm not surprised," Leigh remarked in a faintly humorous voice. "I expect you are wondering where we met."

"It was at Sister North's farewell party," Mandy replied jerkily. Her voice sounded strained and unreal to her ears.

The doctor sighed with relief. "Thank goodness! You do remember. Sister North said you were a friendly person. She advised me to get in touch with you. She thought you might be willing to assist me."

30

Mandy stared at him as if she had not quite taken it in. Her green eyes reflected her state of shock.

"You think I might be able to help you?" she asked uneasily.

"Perhaps . . . it all depends on the circumstances." He laughed awkwardly. "We can't discuss it here. Would you have any objection to meeting me this evening? We could have a meal together. There's a fair amount to talk over."

"Can't you give me some idea of what it is you want?"

The doctor smiled apologetically. "If I do that you will want to know more. Far better do as I suggested."

Mandy hesitated. She had promised to spend the evening at home with Audrey. They were going to ask each other questions about their work in readiness for the exams.

Audrey won't mind if I tell her where I'm going, she thought. After all it would be stupid to refuse an offer of a meal. Audrey will understand that!

"We can make it another evening," the doctor told her.

He had been watching the fleeting expressions of doubt that had flickered across her attractive face. His mouth twitched with amusement. But he took great pains to hide it.

"No!" She smiled faintly. "You have aroused my curiosity. I would rather find out what it is all about today."

"Very well! I should hate to think you were suffering on my account."

She glanced at him suspiciously, caught his quizzing gaze and with an effort pulled herself together. She said fairly evenly: "I finish at six o'clock."

"Make it seven o'clock then. I can't make it later. I'm on call at ten."

"Oh? I thought you were working in Yorkshire."

"Yes, I was there. My mother has been suffering from ill-health so I asked for a transfer. I used to work here."

"Did you?" Mandy asked innocently. She did not want him to know she had been discussing him with a friend.

32

"I had a couple of years here after I qualified."

"Will you mind returning as a house-man?"

"I won't be that this time. I've been given Reggie Brown's place. I expect you have heard that he's left. So I will be another foot up the ladder. I'm going to assist Dr Perkins."

"Rather you than me!" Mandy said lightly.

He laughed. "Yes. He has got an unpleasant reputation. I believe he's not so bad once you get to know him. Anyway I'm pledged now. I've signed on for a year."

"At least the work will be interesting. Reggie found it so. He used to enjoy working in Dr Perkins' laboratory."

The doctor raised his thick dark eyebrows. "You knew Reggie then?"

"Everyone did. He was a friendly person."

"Especially to the nurses?"

Mandy ignored that. "I ought to go back to the ward," she said nervously. "Sister's patience must be running out."

"Sorry to have kept you so long. Tell her it was my fault. Where is the best place to meet you?"

"Perhaps outside the hospital would be best."

Dr Guthrie regarded her unsmilingly. "Sister North said you shared an apartment with another nurse. Apparently you are a good nurse, more serious than others of your age. She also said you would be discreet. I can believe that now."

Mandy smiled. "She said a good deal, didn't she? I had no idea that she noticed me that much!"

His eyes twinkled. "It would be rather difficult not to," he remarked lightly.

"Because of my hair?"

"That, too, of course!" Leigh raised his hand. "See you this evening! I hope I can get there on time. Dr Perkins may decide to work on. I will send you a note if that is the case."

34

I shall keep my fingers crossed, Mandy told herself as she hurried off to her ward. How dreadful if he had to cancel it! I wouldn't have a moment of peace until he contacted me again.

Conscious that Sister was glaring at her forbiddingly, Mandy promptly found something to do. She had no wish to be reported back to her own Sister who had kindly lent Mandy's services.

The unfortunate part about having a previous engagement with Audrey was that Mandy had to explain why she wouldn't be able to keep it. It was something she would rather have done without. Audrey, naturally, was very curious and asked too many unanswerable questions. Any lengthy discussion about the reason for the date only tended to increase Mandy's nervousness.

"It beats me what it can be," Audrey remarked in a puzzled voice before Mandy hurried away to change out of her uniform. "His approach is a new one on me. Most men ask a girl for a date first. They don't make such a thing of it. Perhaps he's trying out something out of the ordinary."

"It's certainly that!" Mandy frowned. "You have it all wrong. He's not interested in me! He wouldn't have suggested meeting me this evening if he could have discussed, whatever it is, this afternoon. You know how difficult it is to talk to anybody when we are working! Sister Morris didn't like it although she was affable enough to the doctor."

"I don't go along with that!" Audrey protested. "His main desire is to place you on his list . . . top of it, I hope!"

Mandy burst into laughter. "Audrey, you idiot! It's not like that at all! I would feel really flattered if I could imagine he was the slightest bit serious. He can't possibly know that I was attracted to him."

"He has made the first move. You can't deny that!" Audrey said stubbornly.

"Sister North told him to get in touch with me. I don't think he even noticed me. It hurts but that's the truth. Let's face it! He's very attractive and obviously prefers women more his own age. How could a slip of a nurse make any impression!"

Audrey grinned. "I know what I would do! This is a golden opportunity. I would play it for all I was worth."

"Just meeting him is all I can manage at the moment," Mandy replied. "I wish I had your confidence."

"It's all very exciting and there's even a soupçon of mystery as well!" Audrey sighed. "I wish it had happened to me! This place is so dull since Reggie left."

"Have you heard from him?"

"Not likely! Diana had a card. She was his latest."

Mandy chuckled. "He was never serious about any of us."

"He was fun. He had to be cautious because of his family," Audrey told her. "Did you know that they gave him a whacking allowance?"

"No. But I did notice that he never seemed to be as hard up as most of the medics," Mandy remarked.

"They are so dull lately."

"Don't forget they have their finals coming up soon. That does make a difference."

Leaving her friend to her brooding thoughts, Mandy hurried into the bathroom taking her dressing-gown and make-up with her. When she emerged she was ready except for choosing something to wear.

"What a problem!" she muttered as she went through her few clothes hanging in the wardrobe. "It will have to be a skirt and top. What does it matter anyway! He won't notice me."

Absent-mindedly, she tucked the light green silk of her blouse into the darker green skirt waist. The result was stunning. She looked very slim and provocative with the sleeves pushed well above her wrists. The stiff wide collar enhanced the smoothness of her slender throat and the beauty of her red-gold hair.

"Will I do?" she asked an enthralled Audrey who had been watching her as she snapped a bracelet over her wrist.

"Absolutely great! I wish I could wear that colour."

Mandy laughed. "I long to wear red! We all want to be different. I always have to tone down what I wear. At least I won't be noticeable in this."

Audrey was grinning at her modest supposition. "That's an understatement if ever I heard one! You will be impossible to miss."

"Oh, do you really think so?" Mandy frowned. "Perhaps I ought to change. I did so want to be unobtrusive."

"That's silly! You look fine. Don't worry! He's seen you before."

"It's that occasion that is worrying me," Mandy replied with a sigh. "He practically ignored me then. Why the sudden change?"

"Sister North had something to do with it. That's obvious. If you don't hurry up and go, I may never discover the answer!"

Dr Guthrie was waiting for Mandy when she arrived slightly out of breath. The streets had been crowded and it had taken her longer than she anticipated.

"Have you been here long?" she asked apologetically. He had not greeted her and his silence was making her nervous.

"I came a few minutes ago. You look so different. I wasn't sure whether it was you." He smiled as he added, "There's no mistaking that hair! That settled it."

"I could dye it, I suppose," she replied dryly, disconcerted by his remarks. He hadn't been very tactful! The colour of her hair had always been a sore point with her.

"You must excuse me," he said as if suddenly aware that he had upset her. "I've only seen you in uniform.

It's quite a transformation!"

He's forgotten my best party dress! Mandy thought, vaguely irritated by his unconcern on that occasion. But of course, he doesn't realise that he made such an impression on me! I really have to be fair and not judge him before I get to know him.

She smiled when he held out his hand.

"Am I forgiven?" he asked.

"You are this time. I'm rather touchy about my hair."

"So I've gathered! That subject will be left well alone. Come on!" he commanded as he took her hand. "My car is parked in the next road. I expect you are hungry. I know I am. We won't go too far."

He took her to a small restaurant a few streets away. Mandy knew of its good reputation. It had been too expensive for the nurses to eat there. So she felt happy that she was going to get a good meal whatever the outcome of the evening might be.

"Do you know this place?" Dr Guthrie asked after they had found an empty table.

"I haven't been here before, but I've heard that the food is good."

"Whatever you order will be tasty, so choose something. I'm settling for a steak." His slate-grey eyes regarded her indulgently as she hesitated. "Would you prefer that, too?"

She nodded. "I would like it well done."

"Very well but do relax! You have tightened up since we arrived."

She smiled faintly. "I was thinking of your pocket."

He glanced at her consideringly. "You are unlike most girls then."

"This is rather different, isn't it?" Mandy said matter-of-factly. "This is not exactly for pleasure."

He frowned. "You needn't put it so bluntly!"

"Sorry! It was a tactless remark."

The waiter approached them and the doctor ordered their meal. They were sipping their wine before Leigh spoke again to Mandy.

"It would be so much easier if you would become less tense. This may be the first of many meals we take together. I don't want there to be any embarrassment between us. Couldn't you try to regard me in a more friendly manner?"

She gave him the ghost of a smile. "I don't feel unfriendly. You are getting the wrong impression of me."

Due to the soothing influence of the wine, Mandy was feeling more in tune with him. She had put aside her fears and uncertainty. It was going to be a lovely evening. Momentarily she had forgotten the purpose behind the invitation.

"We will eat first," Leigh said firmly when the steaks had been set before them. "Discussing anything serious whilst eating can be disastrous."

Mandy gazed at him speculatively. "It grows more mysterious by the minute. Evidently you want me in the best of health! That last statement of yours sounded rather frightening."

He chuckled. "It's nothing of the kind! There's no need to be apprehensive about anything. You only have to say, yes or no.

"I see. It's going to be as easy as that!"

"Eat up! Would you like some more wine?"

Mandy shook her head. She was feeling too sleepy as it was. Something warned her to keep a clear mind. She was prejudiced enough already because she liked him.

She had had nothing to eat since her lunch so she did enjoy the meal. By the time it was finished she felt fully recovered and in command of her faculties.

"That was marvellous!" she told him as they waited for the coffee to arrive.

Leigh nodded. "I'm pleased you enjoyed it."

"Was it a part of your scheme?"

His lips moved in a half smile. "I can

see you don't intend to wait any longer. I have to confess it was a diplomatic move. When you need someone to do a favour for you it is necessary to . . . er . . . "

"Coax them with food, wine and flattery?" Mandy said helping him out.

"Something like that." Leigh grinned ruefully. "You make me feel about an inch high. But I couldn't have talked to you at the hospital. Ten to one we would have been interrupted. And I might have landed you in Sister's black book."

"It *must* be important for you to go to so much trouble!"

Leigh frowned. "It's all due to Dr Perkins. It's his problem. I told you he's to be my boss?"

"Yes." Mandy looked puzzled. "I'm not personally acquainted with him. I don't see how I can help you there."

"The stupid man has got himself into an embarrassing situation. He went to Auckland last year for three months and made some rash promises, never

45

dreaming that they would be taken seriously. It's typical of loners like him. He has few friends here because he's usually unpleasant. He tries to make up for it by exaggerating when he's away from his usual haunts. Only this time he's gone too far!"

"How do you mean?" Mandy asked. She broke off when the waiter appeared with the coffee. "What has he done?"

"He's only offered practically free vacations to all the associates he met out there! Luckily only two have taken advantage of it."

"I don't understand. How could he do that? I thought he lived in a boarding house somewhere near the hospital."

"That's correct. He has no accommodation for anyone."

Mandy gazed at him curiously as she sipped her coffee. She was wondering how she came into all this.

"Has he told you what he is going to do?" she asked.

"Oh, yes! He's doing nothing. He's handed it over to me to sort out."

"That's dreadful! Have they said when they are coming?"

"In two weeks' time according to Perkins. It doesn't give me long, does it?"

"Can't he put them off?" Mandy said sensibly.

"My boss won't hear of it. It's his pride you see," Leigh explained cynically.

Mandy was looking vaguely shocked. "Why did you think I could help you?"

"I told Sister North a more mature person might be able to cope with the situation. I'm afraid I just went along with her suggestion. If you can't suggest anything, well and good. I won't hold it against you."

Mandy bit her lips doubtfully. "Are they young or old?" She inquired when she noticed he was staring at her.

"That I don't know for sure. Perkins said that two women doctors would be arriving. I was to see that they were accommodated, in the hospital if possible."

"That's ridiculous!" Mandy exclaimed.

Leigh nodded. "I know. Perkins is aware of it also."

"I might be able to squeeze in one person but two would be impossible," Mandy said. "I would have to ask Audrey's permission first."

"Is she your room-mate?"

"Yes. She is very understanding. I'm sure she won't mind. We do have a spare bed."

"Sister North promised to help. That was before she decided to leave with her fiancé. It was all arranged at the last minute so it left me stranded. I've been at my wits' end."

Mandy smiled. "I can imagine! I wonder why Sister North suggested me."

"I don't think she had given my problem much thought. After all she had other more important matters to consider. Your presence at her party probably brought you to mind."

Mandy smiled wryly. "That's not very flattering! She could have picked

48

on anyone. My morale is sinking by the minute."

Leigh quickly took her hand and squeezed it. "Please don't give up! You are doing fine! Already you have made one good decision. I was beginning to think I would have to find a small hotel for them."

"That would be well nigh impossible around here. The prices would be terrific!"

"I know that!" Leigh replied darkly.

Mandy thought for a minute or two. Leigh was apparently lost in gloomy consideration of other alternatives. She wanted very much to make his burden lighter.

"I may be able to fix up the other one," she said at last. "Some of the nurses will be going on vacation soon. It all depends on how long the doctors intend to stay."

"I'm afraid that idea is out. They will be here a couple of months at least," Leigh said.

"Heavens, that's a tall order! It would

mean moving them every two weeks. Would they mind that?"

"I haven't a clue. Some people wouldn't mind, others would."

Mandy looked worried. "It would be too difficult. Supposing they are oldish? They will want more comfort than the flat can give. It isn't all that grand!"

"It's very noble of you to offer it. They ought to feel themselves lucky! Accommodation in London is at a premium, especially now," Leigh said gruffly.

"If I was offered free accommodation in New Zealand, I wouldn't grumble too much about the conditions," Mandy remarked. "Perhaps the visitors will feel the same."

"I doubt it. Their standards are probably higher than ours . . . I'm referring to the doctors' apartments."

"London can't be compared with anywhere else," Mandy said stoutly. "They will be so thrilled to be here they won't notice the discomforts."

Leigh chuckled. "You are an optimist!

Thanks anyway. We do seem to be getting somewhere at last. You can sleep one of them."

"Wait a minute!" Mandy said eagerly. "Our rooms are large. If you could find another spare bed we could take the two of them. Audrey could move in with me and that would give the visitors a room to themselves."

"Splendid!" Leigh grinned. "What a clever little nurse you are! I will ask around. Perhaps I could hire one from a struggling comrade who would welcome the chance to make an easy pound or two."

Mandy laughed. "I would hate to think we were tempting one of your hard-working friends to sleep on the floor!" Then she became serious. "Why don't you tell Dr Perkins of your dilemma? He might offer to buy one."

"You must be joking! Obviously you know nothing of the man's true character. The only way I could get a penny from him would be by blackmail. I could threaten to tell his visitors the truth. It wouldn't sound very complimentary, would it? But if I did that, as you no doubt realise, it would be the end of my career!"

"I feel for you!" Mandy said dryly. Relenting a little she added, "There's no doubt, it is an awkward situation for you to be in. I wish I could help more."

"You have solved it almost completely as far as I can see," he told her gratefully. "Sister North couldn't have exceeded your excellent suggestion."

Mandy smiled. "Nurses do have a few brains," she told him cheekily unable to let his remark pass without a sly dig. "I'm aware that you doctors don't credit us with many. That's why we seem unimpressed by your superior knowledge sometimes. You believe we are being insolent."

"It does look that way sometimes." Leigh's mouth twisted in a faint grin. "It doesn't do you any harm to be put in your place occasionally!"

Mandy was taking scant notice of

his teasing. Already her mind was weighing up the pros and cons of finding room for the unexpected guests. It all depends on Audrey, she thought. I do hope she won't object. She is generous about most things but this is a lot to ask.

They were about to leave the restaurant when Leigh commented offhandedly, "There is something I haven't mentioned."

"Oh? Is it important?" Mandy glanced at him doubtfully as they went out into the cool night air.

He took her by the arm and walked her briskly to his car which was in the parking lot behind the building. After they were both settled inside the vehicle, he explained.

"Perkins expects me to ferry the visitors around, see that they have a good time."

"He doesn't want much does he?" Mandy exclaimed with a brief look at his clean-cut profile.

Leigh turned his head and smiled

at her as if pleased and relieved at her support. "I think he's terrified of having much to do with them. It's absurd. Fancy being that scared of people!"

"I bet you wouldn't say that to his face!"

"No way! I have too much respect for the work he does. It amazes me how he can deal with his patients. A doctor has to have some relationship with them."

"He's extremely brusque. I found he left all the pleasantries to the Sister or nurse. We usually calm the patients' fears before they go in to see him. He's fine with the students . . . converses with them quite naturally."

"That's interesting. I've only seen the side he shows to his colleagues. We all get the impression that he can do without us. Of course I'm much younger than he is and haven't had his experience. But it wouldn't hurt him to be sociable."

"The nursing side consider him to

be a peppery individual." She smiled. "We're not being fair to him, are we? Under the surface he may be pleasant and reasonable."

"It takes more imagination than I've got to believe that! I wouldn't risk trying to find out."

"Neither would I!"

Mandy waited until the car was moving before inquiring idly, "I suppose you weren't given their names?"

"I didn't think to ask. It's not important, is it?"

"It might prove a little embarrassing when we first meet. Will you have to go to the airport?"

"I hadn't thought that far ahead," Leigh replied. "I imagine I will have to collect them. But I'm not going to suggest it. It's up to Perkins. If he wants me to go he will have to give me the time off."

"That won't be so bad!" She laughed softly. "I bet you are expecting two attractive females. I would love to see your face if two tough ladies from the backwoods turn up."

"Thanks a lot!" He grinned. "It would be much worse for you in that case. You have to live with them."

"Yes," Mandy said soberly. "I had forgotten."

"Cheer up! It might not be so bad. They may be delightful people." Leigh glanced at her worriedly. "Please don't change your mind about helping me!"

"I won't do that! I promise to put up one of them at least. Audrey will have to agree about the other one. We will be at the hospital all day so what they are like won't affect us unduly."

"Here we are!" Leigh said cheerfully as he steered the car close to the kerb. "This is as far as I can drive you. Do you want me to walk with you?"

"No, thanks. I'm going back to the flat. There's no need for you to come."

Leigh got out of the car and slammed the door. "I will come as far as your street."

It had begun to drizzle. Leigh took her arm and hurried her along. He seemed preoccupied and disinclined for conversation.

Mandy wished she had an umbrella. The rain was dampening and uncomfortable. If she had been alone she would have run to try to save her hair from becoming too wet.

Luckily her road was not far away and Leigh did not linger over the farewell. Mandy had been somewhat nervous about their final parting. She wasn't too sure of what was expected of her.

"I will get in touch with you in a few days," he told her matter-of-factly. "Meanwhile you make the arrangements with your friend."

He sounded too unconcerned and totally unconscious of the impression he was leaving her with. It was almost as if he was now washing his hands of the entire affair.

"Very well. Thanks for the meal," Mandy replied flatly.

He raised his hand in recognition then turned and walked swiftly away across the shiny wet pavement.

Mandy swallowed the hard lump in her throat as she continued to walk home. Somehow it had not been as exciting as she had expected. Suddenly she felt depressed and disillusioned.

I made no personal contact with him. He wasn't impressed with me, she told herself dejectedly. He just wanted a scapegoat, someone to get him out of a mess. Now he's passed his inconvenient task on to me, he's lost interest. I shouldn't have agreed so readily.

Serves me right! she told herself belligerently. I know what the medics are like. I should have left well alone and refused to help. Now I've saddled myself with something I don't really want to be involved in. My common sense tells me I was foolish. And I've drawn Audrey into it also! What is she going to say?

Heavy and dispirited, conscious that she had not behaved wisely, Mandy entered the house and made her way up the stairs to her flat.

3

AUDREY was waiting up for her. The nurse was on early call and ought to have been asleep but she was unable to contain her curiosity.

"How did it go?" she asked eagerly hardly giving Mandy time to take her loose cream jacket off. "What did he say?"

Mandy threw herself on a chair and laughed derisively. Speech seemed beyond her for the moment. But with Audrey staring at her expectantly she had to pull herself together and say something.

"You are going to be awfully disappointed," she said flatly.

"He wasn't bowled over by your outstanding beauty?" Audrey smiled and there was amused mockery in her soft brown eyes.

Mandy shook her head and sighed effectively. "I'm afraid not! He was wrapped up in his own affairs. He was hoping I would help him out of a difficult situation."

"Oh . . . " Audrey sounded downcast and looked at her sorrowfully. Then brightening up a little she asked in a confident voice: "He is going to see you again?"

"Oh, yes," Mandy told her wryly. "I have to let him know whether I succeeded."

"In doing what? You haven't told me where you come in."

Mandy gave her an uneasy glance. "I'm reluctant to tell you because I've involved you as well. And I'm not sure how you are going to react. Naturally, if you object, I won't insist. I shall drop it altogether."

"That's all as clear as mud! For goodness' sake! How can I complain if I don't know what it is! I can't imagine why anything Guthrie wants should involve me. We don't know each other!"

60

"He does now . . . know of you, I mean." Mandy hesitated. "It's all to do with this apartment," she explained reluctantly.

Audrey glanced at her in amusement. "He doesn't want to move in, by any chance?" she asked flippantly.

"No, you idiot!" Mandy hastened to clear up any misunderstanding. "Actually, it was my suggestion but I did say I would have to ask you first."

"Thanks!" Audrey shook her head. "You really are the limit. Perhaps if you stopped feeling guilty you might be able to bring yourself to tell me. Obviously you lost your head and made foolish promises!"

"Something like that." Mandy looked at her seriously. "Only it was Dr Perkins who got carried away not me."

"It's becoming more complicated every minute!" Audrey teased.

Mandy explained, telling her of the great man's rashness and his refusal to face the consequences. Audrey giggled once or twice but Mandy ignored her.

"You know how easy it is to brag when you are in strange company and feeling nervous. I expect that's what happened to him," she said indulgently.

Audrey could scarcely contain her mirth. "I think it's very funny," she gasped.

"Dr Guthrie isn't overjoyed."

"I can understand that! I would feel furious. However did he find the nerve to approach you with his problem?"

"He must have been very friendly with Sister North. She was going to help him. When she found that she couldn't she told him about me."

"I suppose she knew we had a couple of rooms."

"I don't know." Mandy glanced at her thoughtfully. "That side of it is rather a mystery."

"You said two doctors had accepted?"

"That's what I was told. Two women doctors are coming."

Audrey smiled. "You want them to come here."

Mandy gave her a worried look. "That's up to you. I haven't promised anything. I've got two beds in my room. You could share with me and let the other women have your room. We could make it the other way round if you would prefer it."

"Why didn't you come out with it right away? You must have known I wouldn't object!"

"I didn't think you would. But it is a lot to ask of anyone. They are a couple of strangers."

"Does Dr Guthrie think that way also?"

Mandy smiled wryly. "Hardly! You know what the men are like. They do tend to take our support for granted."

"Did he give you a good meal?"

"Marvellous!"

"That's something then!" Audrey sounded faintly sarcastic. "See that he gives me a meal sometime, also!"

"I will do that. You deserve it. Thanks, Audrey! You are a good friend."

"There's nothing to it providing another bed is found. That might prove difficult."

"Dr Guthrie is going to see about that," Mandy told her.

"Two months is a long time," Audrey remarked thoughtfully. "I hope we can get on with them!"

"I expect they will be out most of the time."

Mandy at that point decided not to tell her friend that the doctor was expected to entertain the guests as well. They might prefer to go about on their own. There was no need to anticipate unnecessary worries.

"What about the extra bed-linen?" Audrey asked practically.

"I thought we could ask our landlady to lend us some. She was only saying the other day that she had some she never used. I expect she will have blankets as well. She used to have a large family."

Audrey nodded. "That's another thing. We will have to ask her permission. She might not be too pleased. We don't want to fall out with her!"

"It might give her ideas about doubling up the rooms," Mandy said worriedly. "We are taking a lot of risk!"

"Mrs Torrance only let our rooms because she wanted to have company in the house. Four people all the time would be too much for her."

Mandy sighed with relief. "I'm so glad you aren't upset. By the way aren't you on the early shift?"

"Yes, worse luck!" Audrey smothered a yawn. "I'm off! See you tomorrow. We can discuss it at length then."

Mandy also felt tired but that night sleep evaded her. Her mind kept going over the events of the evening; the words that were exchanged and the considering glances.

I wonder what he really thought of me? she asked herself drowsily. I like him even more now. He's so good-looking. No wonder he's had so many girl friends! I don't believe I made much of an impression. Never mind . . . I will be seeing him again. Perhaps next time . . .

Her sleep was heavy and dreamless. She slept through her alarm and had to hurry so much that she was unable to stop for a cup of tea and some toast.

"Can you find a drink for me?" she whispered to the auxiliary she bumped into as she was entering the ward.

The woman nodded. "Slip into the linen room in five minutes. Do you want anything to eat?"

"Anything will do," Mandy said hurriedly.

Ten minutes had passed before Mandy was able to leave the ward. Luckily Sister had much on her mind and retired to her small office soon after giving her nurses their instructions.

Without incurring anyone's displeasure, Mandy managed to swallow the tea and eat the biscuits the auxiliary had thoughtfully provided. Mandy had often done small services for her so she was delighted to be able to help.

Later, Sister sailed into the ward with Audrey and two other nurses in tow. Audrey winked at Mandy as they passed. She grinned back then regretted it when she noticed Sister's dark frown.

Oh dear! she muttered to herself. I seem to have got out of bed the wrong side this morning. I must marshal my thoughts. I have a full day's work to do and a lecture to attend this evening. I shall never get through it, she decided dismally. Everything is too much today!

"Had a late night, Mandy?" the pupil nurse asked as she was being shown how to check the emergency trolley. "You seem very preoccupied."

"No, not really. I overslept and haven't recovered yet."

"You won't feel right until the coffee break," the girl said sympathetically. "Getting up late upsets the entire day unless you take some time off to relax."

"There's faint chance of doing that!" Mandy replied more cheerfully. Having a little sympathy made all the difference! "I seem to wake up earlier when I go to bed late."

Mandy left her to go in search of Audrey. She found her working with Staff Nurse at a patient's bed.

"What do you want?" Staff said curtly.

"I wondered whether Audrey could go for her break now?" Mandy inquired pleasantly.

"I suppose she might as well go now," Staff replied begrudgingly. "She's not much help here. She's far too fidgety. I don't know what's got into her this morning!"

Audrey grinned at Mandy as they walked the length of the ward. "You are in the same state as I am, aren't you?" she asked in a loud whisper.

"If you mean I can't settle to anything, I am," Mandy replied. "I can't understand why it's affecting us this way!"

"It all goes to show how dull our lives are!" Audrey exclaimed before they got into the crowded lift.

In the canteen Mandy broke her vow never to eat anything during her coffee break. She settled for a buttered scone.

"I'm starving!" she declared almost guiltily as she sat down with her spoils. "Am I making you envious?"

"You know you are!" Audrey said truculently. "It's most unfair!"

"You can have a whacking great lunch after you have finished," Mandy pointed out. "And you can sleep all afternoon. I will have to have a light lunch because I'm working until six o'clock."

"It depends what's on the menu. This isn't a bad canteen. They usually have something fairly appetising."

Halfway through her scone, Mandy asked, "Have you thought over what I said last night? In view of what Staff said, I was beginning to doubt."

"There's no need to get worried. I

haven't changed my mind." Audrey smiled. "You didn't really think I would?"

"I'm in such a state I wouldn't be surprised at anything," Mandy replied. "Shall we ask Mrs Torrance tonight?"

"It will be late when we get in," Audrey reminded her. "Why not leave it until the week-end? She might ask us down to tea on Saturday. She knows we are free in the afternoon."

"Yes. That's a good idea! It will be easier and sound more natural then. We don't want her to think it's terribly important to us so that she feels she must help out." Mandy frowned. "I do hope she won't expect us to pay extra."

"I think she will. She would be within her rights," Audrey replied.

"That's what I thought. I'm beginning to wish I hadn't offered to assist. It seems to be more difficult every minute."

Audrey chuckled. "I was expecting you to get cold feet. You are as bad as Perkins! You can't back out. I won't let you!"

Mandy glanced at her in surprise. "You sound as if you are enjoying all this."

"So would you if you would let yourself go. You get so strained and stiff when anything out of the ordinary happens."

Mandy nodded. "Yes. You are right, as usual. Even Dr Guthrie noticed. He advised me to relax. I do get nervous at the thought of meeting strangers."

"But you are so good with patients! You don't know them until they are admitted."

"That's different! They aren't weighing me up."

"How do you know that?" Audrey laughed. "They have the opportunity and the time."

"They wouldn't dare!" Mandy exclaimed. "If you were ill, would you feel like criticising the nurse who was doing her best to relieve your pain and discomfort?"

Audrey grinned wickedly. "It would depend on the nurse! Seriously, though, I might grumble but I wouldn't criticise. I would be too grateful. It's dreadful to be helpless."

Mandy smiled. "That's very gracious of you! It's time you admitted you were wrong."

"Rubbish! I haven't conceded anything. Patients are strangers. You can't deny that!"

"You would argue all day and night if you had the chance. I agree to differ."

"At least we were of one mind regarding the room sharing," Audrey said.

"Yes," Mandy replied soberly. "I wasn't relishing having to inform Dr Guthrie that I had failed."

Audrey stared at her doubtfully. "He looks handsome enough. What is he really like?"

"I would like to know that myself. He was very pleasant when he took me out. But he could have had a good reason for that seeing that he asked for my help. I'm not sure what he's like normally. Perhaps I shall learn more after the second meeting."

"When is that going to be?"

"Soon I hope. He said he would contact me." Mandy smiled. "Thanks for putting up with me. I know I'm rather on edge." She glanced at her fob watch and frowned. "I will have to go back. Sister's none too pleased with me this morning!"

"I gathered that!" Audrey got to her feet. "I will come with you. There's an interesting case coming in this afternoon. I shall be sorry to miss it."

"Gracious! You are altering! A few months ago you were regarding even ten minutes off as heaven-sent."

Audrey looked rather serious as they made their way towards the lift. "I've become intensely interested in the whys and wherefores of our profession. It struck me very forcibly one day that

I was learning just enough to slide through exams without giving it my full concentration."

"Good for you! But be careful!" Mandy warned her. "You will be deciding to make nursing your career next."

Audrey's jaw jutted defiantly. "What's wrong with that?"

"Nothing! I'm sorry, Audrey. I didn't realise you were serious." Mandy gave her a glance of concern. "You always were more involved than I ever was. I admire women like Sister Morris. They are totally committed."

"Yes." Audrey nodded her head. "I shall be the same one day."

"Haven't you any wish to marry?" Mandy asked curiously.

Audrey gave a short laugh. "That appears no problem at the moment. My relationships never last."

"You might find one that's different one day," Mandy said seriously. "All the same, I think it is a good idea to aim for a career. Something will be achieved. Even if you marry it is useful to have behind you. You never know what might happen."

"That's exactly what I've been thinking," Audrey said. "It will be something important that I've done on my own."

Having settled their futures unanimously, both girls hurried back to the ward. There were two admittances before lunch and the ward seethed with activity. Sister was plagued with doctors and consultants, all expecting her undivided attention. Dr Southwood was one of them. He spent his interval of waiting, happily chatting up any nurse he could buttonhole.

"Are you free this evening, Mandy?" he asked preventing her from rushing off to answer a patient's bell. "No! Sorry, Tony! I have a lecture after I finish."

"You always have something," he grumbled.

Unwilling to waste her sympathy on him, Mandy dashed off. Seconds later, she noticed him talking to Audrey. She smiled to herself as she went to get fresh water for the patient. Apparently that had been overlooked in the general rush.

Tony won't get any change from Audrey, she thought. He's unlucky today. Most of the nurses have to attend the lecture. He might as well give up!

Saturday proved a rewarding day for the two nurses' plans. Their landlady met them on the stairs as they were about to go to the hospital. She asked them whether they were free that afternoon.

"Come in and have some tea with me," she said in a persuasive voice. "I feel like doing some baking. You can help me eat the results of my labours."

Both girls smiled. It was just what they had been waiting for!

"We would love to come Mrs Torrance," Audrey said eagerly. "We finish at twelve today. We can be here at three o'clock."

"No lunch for us today!" Mandy ejaculated as they went out into the sunlight. "That will save us a few pennies."

★ ★ ★

They found their landlady in a good mood when they arrived just before the time they were expected. She had won a small prize with her premium bonds and her delight was catching.

"It is the first time I've ever won anything!" she exclaimed. "I can't believe it!"

"You deserve it," Mandy commented. "This pie is delicious. Could I have some more?"

"You can't ask for more when you still have some on your plate!" Audrey complained. "Your manners are atrocious!"

"I had to get in before you," Mandy said smiling amusedly at Audrey and the landlady.

"I will divide the remainder between you," Mrs Torrance told them. "It does my heart good when I see you tuck in so whole-heartedly."

"Nurses and junior doctors are always hungry," Audrey said. "I think the doctors carry flasks of coffee round with them to keep themselves awake. I expect they practically live on it. Not many of them have the time to eat. They do such long spells on duty."

"It's dreadful!" Mrs Torrance exclaimed. "How do they find time to court a girl and get married?"

Mandy chuckled. "They appear to manage that!"

They were halfway through the meal when Audrey became impatient with the usual flow of conversation. It was high time, she thought to discuss their important issue.

Taking advantage of a lull in the desultory chatting she blurted out, "Do you know much about New Zealand, Mrs Torrance?"

"I have read about it." The woman glanced at her in a startled fashion. "One of my cousins went out there. He never wrote home so we lost touch. Why did you ask? Is it important?"

Mandy chipped in swiftly. "Two friends of mine are coming over for a short visit. They are both doctors."

"That's nice," the landlady remarked. She looked rather puzzled.

Quick to note her expression Mandy hastened to add, "Two women doctors . . . Unfortunately they are nearly as broke as we are so they are looking for reasonable accommodation."

"Yes, I expect they are. London is an expensive city to stay in."

"The thing is, Mrs Torrance . . . " Audrey said awkwardly. "We did wonder if we could do something. We know it's an awful cheek asking you . . . but would you mind if they shared our rooms for a week or so?"

The woman looked at them in frowning silence.

Mandy glanced worriedly at Audrey. But she seemed unable to cope with the situation either.

"We don't mind paying extra for them if that's what is bothering you," Mandy said placatingly.

"It's not that," Mrs Torrance told them. "I wouldn't take any money . . . not because I'm generous . . . It wouldn't be wise. If I did that I would be accepting them as tenants. That's what I would be afraid of. I have to be so careful."

"I see." Mandy glanced at her thoughtfully. "What is it then? I doubt whether they will be noisy or untidy. Audrey and I would see that they behaved reasonably."

The landlady smiled. "It's none of those things. I've nothing against them coming really. I had to give myself time for it all to sink in. It's always nice to see foreign people."

Mandy smiled. "They won't be any different to us."

Both nurses were looking amused

and as relieved as they felt. Before they left they had arranged for some extra bed linen and a spare bed which apparently was tucked away in the jumble room.

"You need somewhere to store odds and ends," Mrs Torrance explained. "The room is small but it comes in handy. I don't like to part with everything."

"I don't know how she gets in there!" Audrey remarked laughingly as they returned to their rooms on the third floor. "It's packed to the door!"

"She was extremely obliging," Mandy said gratefully. "I will have to get in touch with Dr Guthrie. He won't have to find another bed now."

Audrey said worriedly, "She didn't ask us how long they will be staying."

"Let's cross that bridge when we come to it. They may be so charming that she will be putty in their hands."

Audrey chuckled. "Supposing they are impossible to deal with? You will have a lot of explaining to do!"

Mandy nodded. "I know. I hate telling lies, even white ones. They never seem to stop there. One leads to another. Perhaps we ought to have told her the truth."

"She would never have agreed then! She would have thought you were foolish to take on the responsibility."

Mandy sighed. "Sometimes I feel the same. I do hope it all goes smoothly!"

★ ★ ★

Dr Guthrie was feeling as anxious as the nurses were. His boss was keeping him very busy and he had not been able to find the time to get in touch with Mandy. He wanted to find out if she had been successful about the room. All his plans hinged on that.

If Mandy let him down then he would have to approach Dr Perkins and ask him to supply the money for the hotel bookings. It was the last thing he wanted to do. If Perkins refused, the situation could become tricky. No way could he, himself, afford to pay hotel bills.

I could tell him to find some other mug to do his dirty work, he told himself truculently. He was watching the great man demonstrating to a group of students in the examining room and was taking the opportunity to have a quiet think. I don't want to chuck my future away. Perkins could do me untold harm. But if I keep in his good books, his favourable reference will prove invaluable.

I could emigrate, I suppose, he mused gloomily. I would still need someone to recommend me. A good word from Perkins would do wonders. He is head and shoulders above my previous chiefs. I shall have to knuckle under and find the money somewhere. Perhaps I could explain to the visitors . . . if they are a decent pair they might understand . . . No! What am I thinking of? I couldn't do that! I might just as well commit suicide now and refuse to co-operate.

He was in no mood to be pleasant to anyone when he finally extricated himself from Dr Perkins' watchful eyes. Tony Southwood, as bland as ever, pinned him down when he was trying to relax in the doctors' leisure room. With careless aplomb the selfish young man aired his views concerning the new influx of student nurses.

"Some of them aren't bad, not by any standards!" he exclaimed loudly.

"Keep your voice down!" Leigh muttered as heads were raised from their reading matter. "Not everybody is interested in your choice of females."

"None of them are a patch on Nurse Greenwood," an unabashed Tony told him in a voice only slightly less exuberant.

Leigh feigned indifference. "Really? I haven't seen her lately."

"I was on her ward this morning."

"Which one is that?" Leigh asked.

"Women's medical. They were very busy there. Sister Blake's charming façade had slipped. The nurses were scurrying hither and thither. None of them had a chance to speak to me!"

"Too bad! That was terrible for you," Leigh said sarcastically.

Tony glanced at him suspiciously. "It was. What with exams and lectures, the nurses aren't much fun these days."

Unable to listen to his colleague's inane remarks any longer, Leigh left him. Tony's reference to Mandy had irritated him. He had been scarcely aware of his feelings toward the nurse but now he was conscious of an urgency to keep her isolated from his fellow doctors. He didn't want her to associate with any of them!

He needed to see her. The importance regarding the accommodation paled beside his other reason. He wanted to see those clear, green eyes light up when he spoke to her. If she smiled that would be another bonus. She had captured his imagination with her good looks and intelligence.

She might not be as pleased to see me, he told himself cautiously. I shall have to tread warily.

It was rather a nerve expecting her to put herself out for someone she didn't know. Someone she might not even like! Obviously, she was a kind and considerate person for she hadn't refused to help. But she might have changed her mind by now. She'd had time to think it over.

I wish I had never asked her, he thought gloomily. It was a mood he seemed to be unable to shake off lately. Why should she be inconvenienced? The doctors might be terribly boring and a nuisance. None of them got much spare time . . . Mandy must be wishing him further!

He became increasingly on edge as he went over what he would say to Mandy. I will tell her not to bother, he finally concluded. I would rather have her friendship. It's going to make things difficult if I'm in her debt.

At least I know she is still in the same ward, he mused. There was a chance of her going to surgical. I remember she feared having to work with Sister Winley who has a reputation for being a dragon.

It's no good! I won't be able to settle to anything until I have seen her, he thought irritably. He glanced at his watch with frowning concentration. I might as well go now ... use up some of my lunch break. Perhaps I will be able to work more readily this afternoon.

On the other hand, if it's bad news, I might as well give up, he reflected with a heavy sigh. I've almost got used to this daily feeling of dread. And it is all so unnecessary! That's what makes it so infuriating. Why didn't Perkins use a little diplomacy? He needn't have been so generous! But then he never dreamed his offers would come home to roost!

Mandy was on the point of going to lunch. But as Sister had asked her to stand in for Staff Nurse, she was staying on for another half an hour.

She was feeling a little fed up because

she would miss the chance to chat to Audrey. It was small pleasures like that, that made the work seem lighter and the day pass more swiftly. However as it turned out, the change in her lunch hour was to prove more rewarding than she could have anticipated.

She was in Sister's office answering the house telephone when Dr Guthrie walked in and closed the door behind him. He looked somewhat agitated. Mandy was able to glean that much as she glanced across at him.

4

MANDY finished speaking and replaced the receiver. She wrote down the message, which was important, on Sister's note-pad. Then she looked up.

"I was hoping to see you soon," she exclaimed giving him a bright smile. "Things have been happening and I wanted to put you in the picture."

Leigh gave her a startled glance. "Are they good or bad?" he inquired anxiously.

She laughed. "Don't look so alarmed! I think they are good. Firstly, Audrey has offered to move in with me. That leaves a room free for the two visitors."

"What about your landlord?"

"Landlady!" Mandy corrected him. "That's okay, too. She has given her consent. And she is going to lend us the bed linen."

"That's great . . . really great!" Leigh exclaimed. He looked so relieved that Mandy was unable to suppress her laughter. She had been unaware that he had been relying on her that much!

"Were you scared I wouldn't be able to help you?" she asked.

"Wouldn't you have been?" he countered.

"I suppose so," she replied doubtfully. Then she smiled. "I can't see myself taking on Dr Perkins' responsibilities."

"I ought to have had more sense," he said moodily.

"I don't agree!" Mandy was instantly sympathetic. "You had a very good reason. You had to think of your future."

He smiled and moved close enough to her so that he could rest his hands on her shoulders. He pressed them gently unconscious that he was embarrassing her.

"You are a dear and kind person," he said, the warmth in his voice conveying more meaning to his actual words.

"You have saved me from Perkins' sarcasm and wrath. Thanks a million!"

"It wasn't that good," Mandy replied awkwardly. She stepped back so that he was forced to release her. "Audrey is the one you ought to thank. She is the noble one."

"I'm sure you are right." Leigh was regarding her with a faint smile playing about his mouth. "The next few weeks are going to be most enjoyable."

"I hope so," Mandy replied feeling puzzled. Perhaps the prospect of escorting two females from overseas was beginning to tantalise!

Leigh was frowning. "I had forgotten the bed. I will have to see about that."

"There's no need to do that," Mandy said quickly. "Mrs Torrance, that's our landlady, has offered to provide us with a spare one. We can move it into Audrey's room."

"You appear to have thought of everything!" Leigh grinned happily. "You have left me nothing to do.

What efficiency!"

"I would have thought that shepherding them around would be the most difficult part," Mandy said. "Has Dr Perkins said anything about meeting them at the airport?"

"Not so far! He gives me the impression that he's forgotten all about them. But that may be all a pretence."

"Why don't you ask him?"

"He would bite my head off!" Leigh smiled ruefully. "On the other hand if I remain silent I will get blamed for negligence."

Mandy chuckled. "You can't win, can you?"

"Not with my boss!" Leigh glanced at her thoughtfully. "You mentioned your friend, Audrey. I think I ought to take you both out. I expect you would prefer to go for a meal. It would be just a gesture to show my appreciation."

"Audrey would like that."

He frowned. "I was hoping you would enjoy it also."

"Of course, it will be a treat for

both of us!" Mandy glanced at him apologetically. "I'm deputising for Staff Nurse. I must go back to the ward and see what is happening."

Leigh nodded. "Thanks for talking to me. I'm afraid Perkins keeps me pretty busy day and night. But next Thursday, he's going to Norfolk. Could you two arrange for a free evening?"

"I'm sure we can," Mandy said hurriedly.

"Make it the same time and place as last time," he said as he opened the door for her. "Someone is trying to attract your attention! I will be off. Take care!"

When Staff Nurse returned and she was able to go to lunch, Mandy could still feel the pressure of Leigh's fingers on her shoulders. Or was it imagination that a burning sensation had remained there and wouldn't die away?

Oh dear, I do like him, Mandy reflected wistfully as she wended her way towards the lift. He can't be all that keen on me though. He didn't ask me out for another date. The one with Audrey won't count although I shall enjoy it. Audrey will be thrilled to learn that she's going to have a really good meal!

She sighed as she walked into the empty lift and pressed the button. It will probably be the end of our association, she decided forlornly. He won't need me to take two women out. It's more than likely that he will want to be on his own.

"It's no more than he should do!" Audrey stated bluntly when Mandy gave her the good news. "We are going to a lot of trouble for him."

"He realises that. And I pointed out that it would be you who was going to suffer the most."

"I bet he didn't know how to answer that," Audrey remarked with a laugh.

"He didn't say anything at the time but later he gave us the invitation. So my pointed remark must have sunk in."

"I can't say that I'm not delighted.

Food from any quarter is a treat. And if it's going to be the same restaurant he took you to, we will have a good meal. I can't remember when I was taken out last for a three course dinner."

"You have a short memory!" Mandy told her. "Reggie gave you one a few days before he left."

"That was ages ago!" Audrey grinned wickedly. "It's going to be very interesting. I shall be able to see for myself what the doctor thinks of you!"

"Cheeky!" Mandy smiled confidently. "You will be disappointed. He's a dark horse. I find it difficult to be at ease with him. He's not going to allow you to read his innermost thoughts."

"You can't be positive about that. I have an instinct in such matters," Audrey said, refusing to be beaten.

The days passed fairly uneventfully with life at the hospital carrying on as usual. Both girls settled down to study hard for their exams.

The evening out with Dr Guthrie

passed without incident. He gave them both a good meal and escorted them home immediately afterwards. Mandy thought that it was all disappointing. They could have lingered over their coffee to chat. But when the doctor informed them that he was on call later that evening, neither girl could complain.

"Why didn't he choose another night when he was completely free?" Audrey grumbled afterwards. "It was almost as though he was pleased he had an excuse to get rid of us."

"Obviously it was something of a duty for him," Mandy agreed. "I suppose now his worries have evaporated he's not concerned about us."

"That's it in a nutshell!" Audrey said.

"I'm beginning to change my mind about him. He's not as affable as he seemed at first."

Audrey frowned at her serious face. "Don't forget, he does have a very busy life! Dr Perkins' assistants never last long. He quickly wears them out."

Mandy smiled. "Yes. I've heard that. Leigh did look tired. And when he arranged the date he may not have known he would have to be on call that evening."

"I think it's best to forget all about it," Audrey said sensibly. "Push all the doctors right out of our minds. We have enough worries at the moment. These exams are important!"

"Yes. It will be fun being known as 'Staff', won't it?"

Her friend looked horrified. "Don't mention that word! It's terribly unlucky! Let's wait and see what happens."

"I'm not going out with anyone until they are over." Mandy said firmly.

"What if Dr Guthrie asks for a date?"

"He will be turned down. Only a summons from Buckingham Palace will move me!"

Audrey giggled. "Brave words! Come on! We will be late for Mr Stevens' class. It's theory first then practical. I learn more from his sessions than from anyone else. I don't want to miss it."

Dr Guthrie was hovering outside the lecture room when the two nurses left to go home. He appeared rather distraught and pulled them both aside more roughly than was necessary.

"Sister Blake told me you were here," he explained hurriedly. "I have been waiting for some time."

"It must be important then," Mandy said. "Has something happened to upset you?"

Leigh shrugged his shoulders in disgust. "It's Perkins! He's had another letter. Apparently the trip has been delayed."

Mandy frowned. "Does it matter? When are they coming?"

"Middle of next month, according to my boss."

"That's nearly three weeks away!" Audrey exclaimed.

"Yes." Leigh looked uneasily at

Mandy. "I'm very sorry. It will upset your plans."

"Actually, it's much better for them to come later," she said cheerfully. "Our exams start next week. We don't really want to think of anything except them."

"I see!" Leigh's expression lightened. "Naturally you won't want to be concerned with anything else. The exams will be over by the time the New Zealanders arrive. You were taking a chance!"

"We had to do that," Audrey said rather sharply. "Obviously we couldn't ask for the dates to be changed so we just got on with it." She smiled. "We might not have been very good company for a few days."

"At least they would have had a room to themselves," Mandy said, uneasy about her friend's blunt manner.

Leigh gave her a grateful look. "It was good of you to offer to have them in the circumstances. I had no idea your exams were so near."

"We did play with the idea of telling Dr Perkins to see to his own visitors," Audrey said lightly. "If it happens again we won't be so obliging."

Leigh looked at her in alarm. "Don't do that! I'm sure it won't occur again."

Mandy smoothed the ruffled waters by saying mildly, "Audrey is a great tease. Take no notice of her."

"I see," Leigh replied in a relieved voice. "Are you going back to your apartment? I will walk back with you if you wish."

"We aren't going home yet," Audrey said quickly. "We have several things to discuss with the other nurses. They are waiting for us in the first aid room."

Leigh nodded, turned on his heel and left them. Mandy watched his tall, white-coated figure gradually disappear down the corridor. She was dismayed at his sudden exit and blamed Audrey for her curt dismissal.

"You needn't have been so sharp!" she complained. "It was kind of him to offer."

"He irritated me," Audrey replied. "He gets in such a flap when things don't go his way."

"He was concerned about how it was going to affect us. That was thoughtful of him. He needn't have said anything. We would have just gone on waiting."

"I suppose he was trying to be helpful," Audrey conceded begrudgingly.

"We can concentrate on our exams now. We won't have to bother about getting the room ready," Mandy said in a satisfied voice.

★ ★ ★

Two weeks later both nurses were facing each other at a table in the canteen. They were gloomily sipping a belated coffee. Neither of them was making an attempt to brighten their outlook.

"It was awful," muttered Audrey with a glazed expression in her brown eyes. "I couldn't answer any of the questions coherently. When I saw that examiner I just froze to the floor."

"Yes, that's what I did," Mandy agreed unhappily. "It took me ages to find my tongue. When I did come to, I babbled a lot of nonsense that came into my head. I didn't mind the examiner so much. It was the others who were sitting there taking notes who unnerved me."

"I was surprised I was there so long! I really did expect to be told to go . . . that they were finished with me."

"Perhaps we did so well on the theory that they suffered a few mistakes with the oral."

Audrey laughed shortly. "Not a chance! But we can't alter anything now. We shall have to resign ourselves to failure."

"There is one comforting thought!" Mandy smiled and went on more cheerfully, "All the other nurses believe they have failed also."

"Yes . . . I see what you mean," Audrey said, pulling herself up straight in her chair. "Some will pass."

"I scarcely think Maxwell and Greenwood will be amongst them," Mandy said dejectedly.

"We will *not* speak of it again!" Audrey said firmly. "Have you heard from Dr Guthrie?"

"No. I didn't expect to. I imagine it won't be long now. We ought to get the room ready. That will take our minds off the exam results."

"Mrs Torrance has asked us to tea on Saturday."

Mandy nodded. "That will give us the chance to ask her for the extra bed. I expect she has got it ready for us."

"If we knew when the visitors were going to arrive we could get some extra food in," Audrey said sensibly.

The two girls had the use of a small kitchen on the top floor. The refrigerator was small but it did have a freezing compartment. There was enough room to store a few packets.

"I will have to draw some money from my building society," Mandy remarked thoughtfully. "We can't expect our guests to exist on our normal fare!"

"Why don't you ask Dr Perkins?" Audrey said flippantly.

Mandy laughed. "Can you see me doing that?"

"They are his guests. He ought to pay for them."

"Perhaps he will. But I'm not asking him!"

Mandy did not have to go out of her way to find Dr Guthrie. She discovered him in Women's Medical the next morning. He was standing at a patient's bedside with a group of students around him.

She cast a glance in Sister's direction and noticed that she was talking to Dr Perkins. Evidently, he had left his round for Dr Guthrie to do.

Leigh was deftly giving an injection and explaining why he was doing so when Mandy approached. It took him a few seconds to become aware of her. He shook his head and receiving the signal correctly, she moved on.

It was difficult to find things to do without attracting her seniors' eyes. She came upon a screened bed and disappeared behind the curtains. There she could see but not be seen.

"Not another consultant!" the woman in the bed grumbled. "I've had my bed tidied three times this morning!"

"Relax! He's not come to see you, Mrs James," Mandy assured her. "I'm just keeping out of the way."

"Best thing to do with some of them," the woman replied in bored tones and closed her eyes.

Mandy smiled to herself. Consultants were the cream of the medical profession, yet patients rarely took to them. They were too far removed. And too much grandeur surrounded their visits. Sisters sailed round behind them passively attending to their slightest wish. Even the young doctors behaved awkwardly. Polite and reserved, they only spoke when they wanted to ask some pertinent question. And the nurses, sometimes overawed, did not dare to address any of them unless Sister gave firm instructions.

Mandy had to admit that there were one or two consultants who did not fit into this pattern. They were more friendly and set their patients at ease. They spoke to them naturally even easing a joke or two into the bedside pleasantry. This altered the students' attitude also. They became more relaxed and probably took in more that was said than they might have done if they were in a nervous state.

Dr Perkins did not fit into the latter category. So, Mandy remained hidden. In ten minutes he and his entourage had gone. Sister immediately urged her band of diligent nurses to resume their normal duties and the work carried on as usual.

Not so for Mandy, though! She had caught sight of Dr Guthrie. He had not followed Dr Perkins and the students out of the ward. Mandy guessed that he was trying to attract her attention whilst Sister was busy with the other nurses. Feeling doubtful and nervous, she hurried across to the swing doors where he was standing.

"Come outside a minute," he muttered quietly.

He opened the door for her. Mandy hesitated but had to comply when he gave her a gentle shove.

"You will get me into trouble!" she complained. "Sister noticed me come out. What is it? It will have to be a good reason!"

"It is important enough! I wanted to let you know before but I couldn't get away from Perkins. You know what he's like! I will have to be quick. He will be sending out a search party for me."

"And I shall get a reprimand from Sister! You do choose the most awkward places to meet!"

"I'm sorry!" Dr Guthrie looked apologetic. "But I had to tell you as soon as possible. Would you believe it? The visitors have already arrived!"

Mandy looked blank. "It's too soon,

isn't it?" she asked in a dazed voice.

Leigh shook his head. "Not really. I expect you are confused because of your exams."

"Maybe! But I did think it would be next week."

"Perhaps you are right. I feel rather vague about it myself. Anyway Perkins mucked it up as usual! I was supposed to meet them. I was rather looking forward to that. Would you believe it? He went himself!"

Mandy smiled. "It does take a little imagination. I wouldn't have thought he would have had the nerve."

"Apparently he was more or less forced to go. I was out on one of his errands when he received a phone call from the airport. He said they asked him to meet them personally."

"That's not surprising!" Mandy exclaimed. "Where are they now?"

"Perkins has left them in one of his consulting rooms. I have to give him a hand with them later."

"Haven't you met them yet?"

"No. My boss seems highly amused about something." Leigh frowned. "I don't trust that man! He's up to something, I'm pretty sure."

Mandy gave him a worried glance. "I don't see what I can do at the moment."

"I realise that! I just thought you ought to be aware of the recent event. I wanted to prepare you."

"Thanks," Mandy said flatly. "It would have been a shock to find them on our doorstep! Their room is ready. You can bring them along this evening."

Leigh seemed uneasy. "How about sooner, if I have to?"

"Mrs Torrance will be there. She will show them to the room. Don't worry! I'm sure it will be all right."

"I'm not worried about Mrs Torrance. It's Perkins! I'm feeling distinctly wary about his next move."

"I must go back to the ward!" Mandy said firmly. "Sister will have me on the carpet. She might even make me stay late tonight!"

"We can't have that!" Leigh ejaculated. "Tell her I was discussing a patient's diet with you."

Mandy looked horrified. "I can't do that! She is my senior!"

"No, it wouldn't be very clever. I wasn't thinking." Leigh gave her a smiling glance. "You could say I wasn't feeling well and asked for your assistance."

Mandy's eyes brightened. "That's better," she exclaimed with some relief. "You were so bad I had to help you along the corridor where I handed you over to one of your colleagues."

Leigh grinned. "You needn't elaborate so much. It's a bit thin but I guess it will do."

"It will have to," Mandy said rather grimly. "If it doesn't you might find yourself in hot water."

"You won't betray me."

"You are very sure of yourself," Mandy retorted. "You've not seen me when I'm cross."

"I can't wait for the day!" He replied flippantly. "See you later, I expect," he added before he turned away.

Sister gave Mandy a steady glare when the nurse entered the ward. Sometimes it wasn't necessary to say anything. A look was sufficient to cause most nurses to quake in their shoes. However, as Mandy usually got on well with Sister Blake, she took no pleasure in upsetting her.

Diets were very important on the medical ward. And they caused quite a few headaches for the staff when the physicians constantly tried out their own pet theories. Mandy spent most of the afternoon working with the auxiliary nurse who had not had much experience dealing with the diets.

"You can't go far wrong if you sterilise all your utensils before you use them," Mandy told her. "I know some of you try to bypass that but I wouldn't want to be in your shoes if something went wrong."

"Do the diets get mixed up

sometimes?" the girl asked.

"Most unlikely!" Mandy said firmly. "That's why I'm showing you how to read individual sheets. It's quite easy if you concentrate."

The auxiliary sighed. "There is such a lot to learn. I will never remember all of it."

"Yes, you will," Mandy said encouragingly. "We all have to start somewhere. And we all lose confidence at times."

"I can't believe you do," the girl said.

Mandy smilingly went on her way. She had to stand back to allow a porter with a stretcher case through the swing doors of her ward. A staff nurse from casualty was walking alongside holding the drip. The patient could not be left alone. But as soon as she had handed the new intake over to Sister Blake the staff nurse left to return to casualty.

"Nurse Greenwood! For once you are in the right place at the right time!" Sister ejaculated. "Help me get her into bed!"

The woman was heavy and they had to ease and roll her from the stretcher on to the bed with another nurse taking care of the drip. Sister and Mandy were breathing heavily by the time they had transferred the patient. The doctor arrived on the scene shortly afterwards.

It was a different Dr Guthrie to the one Mandy knew. He was cool, concise and remote. His examination after reading what casualty had to say, was swift and sure.

"Apparently, she collapsed in the street," he remarked to Sister. Mandy was ignored as he continued to explain.

Mandy knew that it was nothing unusual. She was used to being in the background. To most of the senior doctors, the nurses scarcely existed unless some task had to be done.

"To me it's pretty obvious that she's had a slight stroke. But I won't let it rest there. I will ask for Dr Perkins' opinion.

These cases need careful handling. So I won't prescribe until we are sure. Meanwhile, she is not to be left alone. And temperature and pulse taken every hour, Sister!"

"You will require a blood sample?"

"That's correct, Sister. You know the drill!" Dr Guthrie sounded curt.

"Yes, Doctor." Irene Blake's voice would have frozen a lesser man.

Mandy could sense the undercurrents. These two had a closer relationship than she had realised. Sister's voice had been so coldly sarcastic, almost insolent. Mandy had never heard her speak in such a way to anyone before.

Leigh looked much paler than usual as he leaned over the patient once more. When he straightened up he gave Sister a level glance.

"You are entitled to your opinion, Sister," he said curtly. "I am sticking to mine."

"As yet I haven't ventured one," she replied stiffly.

"You didn't have to. I know full well

what you would have advised!" Leigh said tersely.

"I wouldn't presume to do that!" she retorted. For a brief moment anger blazed in her eyes.

"Keep her warm!" Leigh said flatly.

He pulled back the curtain screen with a fierce jerk and stalked from the ward. Mandy glanced anxiously and curiously at Sister Blake. On her lips a faint twisted smile was beginning to appear. And it was evident that she considered she had scored over Dr Guthrie. Mandy could make no sense out of it at all.

"Get on with it, nurse!"

The sharp reprimand brought Mandy quickly to her senses. For a moment or two, she had forgotten the patient! Swiftly she set about making the woman comfortable after she had taken the blood sample.

It was much later that she recalled the strange incident and her conclusions set her wondering. What was it between those two? There was dislike on Sister's side, obviously. Mandy had never seen her on the offensive before. She had been very angry! It was almost as if she had wanted to hurt him!

Mandy was distinctly puzzled. But she soon had other more personal matters to consider. Sister Blake's small mystery was forgotten after the shock Mandy received on arriving back at her flat. Her landlady came out of her room to greet her as soon as she opened the front door.

"My dear, your friends have arrived!" she exclaimed. "I didn't quite know what to do so I gave them some tea."

Mandy glanced at her in a dazed fashion. "The visitors, of course!" she ejaculated. "That was kind of you. How long ago was that?"

"About an hour, I think. You know how time passes when you talk." Mrs Torrance was looking slightly puzzled. "Isn't Audrey with you?"

"No. She had some shopping to do." Mandy moved towards the landlady's

116

sitting-room. "Is it all right if I go in?" she asked politely.

Mrs Torrance shook her head. "They aren't down here now. After they had had their tea they seemed restless so I took them upstairs. I knew which room was going to be their bedroom."

"I'm so sorry," Mandy said apologetically. "It must have been a nuisance for you."

"I didn't mind but I was somewhat surprised. Perhaps they behave differently in New Zealand."

Mandy frowned unable to understand her meaning. "Did Dr Guthrie come with them?" she asked.

"No. That wasn't the name," Mrs Torrance stared at her doubtfully. "One of them called him Perky."

"Oh, no!" The shock had made Mandy's face whiten. "He can't be here!"

"Are you all right, Mandy?" Mrs Torrance's worried voice pulled the girl together.

"Yes. I've been rushing. Thanks,

Mrs Torrance! I will see to things now."

Mandy dashed up the stairs as if she had not one moment to lose. Mrs Torrance was left with an astounded expression on her kindly face.

5

MANDY hesitated when she reached the landing. She could hear nothing so opened the door into the kitchen first.

A young man was washing his hands at the sink unit. He was blond with big shoulders and when he straightened, Mandy could see that he was tall.

"Hello!" she said in an astonished voice. "Who are you?"

"Leslie Davis." His grin was wide and friendly. "You must be Mandy!"

She nodded, feeling dazed and bewildered as she watched him hasten to dry his hands. When he had thrown down the towel he took hold of both her hands and shook them vigorously.

"I can't tell you what a treat it is to be here!" he exclaimed in a voice which had a trace of a drawl. "It's a real big favour, you are doing us. Neither of us wanted to come as tourists. This is much more friendly."

"That's right!" Another deep voice drawled behind Mandy. "This is exactly the kind of environment we need."

"Really?" Mandy stammered. She was completely disarmed by their friendliness and overwhelmed by their masculine presence. Both of them were so big!

"Do you play rugby?" she asked inanely for her mind was bogged down by shock.

The blond one laughed. "Why do we always get asked that? Yes we do occasionally, when we find the time. Our profession doesn't give us much of that."

"Yes, of course!" Mandy replied hurriedly. "I had forgotten you were doctors." She stared at them curiously. "How did you know my name?"

"The kind lady downstairs told us," the dark-haired one explained smilingly. "We gathered from what she said that we were supposed to know you. Don't worry! We were tactful. She has a snapshot of you and Audrey on her bureau."

Mandy nodded. "I see! What have you done with Dr Perkins? I thought he was with you."

The two men exchanged glances and chuckled.

"Perky couldn't stomach us for too long," the blond man said in an amused voice. "Apparently he had a very important appointment. He rushed off soon after we arrived."

Mandy nodded. "He is an important man."

Silently she was debating what she ought to do. The shock of finding two men instead of the women she had been expecting was still bemusing her mind. She was finding it difficult to think coherently. What was she to do with them?

She prayed for Audrey to return and revive her flagging spirits. Perhaps she ought to explain to them . . . they seemed very reasonable . . . but would it be wise? Her brain seemed numbed by the ghastly mistake that had been made.

No wonder Mrs Torrance was surprised, Mandy thought. We told her two women friends were coming. Why did Dr Perkins bring them here?

"What has happened to your luggage?" she asked, suddenly aware that they were staring at her curiously.

"We brought that along with us," the blond one told her cheerfully. "We travel light."

"No wonder you seem puzzled," the dark-haired giant remarked. "We haven't introduced ourselves. At least I haven't. I'm Vivien Straker."

"Vivien and Leslie . . . I'm beginning to understand," Mandy muttered quietly.

The men looked at her in frowning silence. When footsteps were heard on the stairs, Mandy heaved a sigh of relief. At last! she thought . . . another few minutes and I would be blurting out the truth!

Fortunately it wasn't only Audrey

who appeared. She had Dr Guthrie with her.

Mandy hastened to introduce them all as they squeezed into the small kitchen. She could almost feel the shock waves that emanated from Leigh and Audrey.

Leigh was the first to recover. "We can't talk here," he said. "Shall I go with you to your room? We needn't detain the girls any longer. I expect they have plans for this evening."

"Sure! Let's do that," Leslie said agreeably. "We don't want to inconvenience anybody."

"Dr Perkins asked me to give you any assistance you might need," Leigh explained as he led the two men away.

When they had gone, both girls rushed to the safety of Mandy's room and closed the door.

"Not inconvenience us!" Audrey exclaimed in a horrified voice. "What a fine kettle of fish! Who is responsible for such a terrible blunder?"

"Dr Perkins is, I imagine." Mandy

sighed as she sat down on one of the beds. "We can't have them staying here!"

"Whatever did Mrs Torrance say?"

"She took it very well." Mandy smiled. "She actually gave them tea!"

"My word! I bet they loved that!" Audrey had a sudden thought. "How did they find their way here?"

"Dr Perkins brought them."

"He didn't! He knows all about us then!"

"Leigh told him we had offered to give up a room."

"How could he!" Audrey ejaculated in disgust.

"He had to give some explanation," Mandy said. "I believe that Dr Perkins genuinely thought they were women doctors. At first, that is . . . When he received his last communique, Leigh said he looked amused."

"The monster!" Audrey exclaimed indignantly. "It would serve him right if we marched them back to him and left him to sort it out."

Mandy chuckled. "Which one will you tackle?"

"They are big, aren't they!" Audrey grinned. "Oh, deary me! You must have been on pins and needles when you discovered them."

"I was flabbergasted! I didn't know what to say. They probably thought I was dim-witted!"

Before Audrey could reply there was a knock on their door. The nurses glanced at one another in alarm.

"Come in! It's not locked," Mandy called out.

Dr Guthrie eased himself into the room as if afraid to use any more space than was necessary. He was extremely nervous and cleared his throat noisily. It was obvious that his courage had failed him for he could not meet their questioning eyes.

"It won't do, of course," he stammered. "I'm terribly sorry! Perkins did tell me that two women doctors were coming. I do hope you aren't blaming me."

"We surmised that it was Perkins' mistake. But the fault is yours also," Audrey said crisply. "The two specimens who are next door hardly tie in with what you told us to expect!"

"Audrey! There's no need to be rude," Mandy said. Her kind heart was getting the better of her first reservations about the contretemps. She was recovering from the initial shock and was viewing the situation more reasonably.

"You have to admit, we have been taken in," Audrey protested.

"It is unfortunate. But they seem to be pleasant men," Mandy said. "It's not their fault. They believe it's all been arranged for them."

Leigh threw her a grateful glance. "I've explained to them that they can't stay here," he said hurriedly. "The only drawback is that I shall have to leave them here until I can find somewhere for them to sleep."

"Have you anything in mind?" Audrey asked pertly.

Leigh frowned. "Not at the moment!"

"You could hand them over to your boss."

"Audrey is only joking," Mandy said quickly.

Leigh smiled faintly. "I agree with Audrey. I wish I had enough nerve to do just that. Perkins needs teaching a lesson."

"The trouble is that you would be upsetting the visitors if you did that," Mandy said unhappily. "We owe our landlady an explanation. I'm going downstairs now to tell her the truth."

"I will come with you," Leigh said. "It's my fault that we have caused her so much trouble."

"She won't see it like that," Mandy assured him.

She was right. Mrs Torrance was more understanding than they deserved. She even gave them some sound advice.

"I've been young myself. You seem to forget that," she said with a smile of indulgence. "Mind you, I have to agree that you have got yourselves into a muddle. I had a suspicion that the Perky chap was up to no good. He kept smiling and wouldn't stay to tea."

Mandy had to bite her lips to prevent her sudden grin from showing. To refuse tea was a cardinal sin in the landlady's eyes.

Leigh was attempting to explain. "Dr Perkins is my boss. He often gives me tasks to do which really he ought to bother about himself. The New Zealanders are his problem. He invited them to stay with him not believing that they would ever come."

"I'm beginning to understand. They aren't friends of the two nurses!"

Mandy said unhappily, "I'm sorry, Mrs Torrance, especially about the fairy story I told you."

The woman chuckled. "You must have had a shock same as I did! I thought it was peculiar. Audrey and Mandy don't usually make mistakes . . . not about things like that!"

Audrey smiled. "I'm thankful you

128

have such a high opinion of us. We would never have arranged for them to stay if we had known."

"I believe that. If I didn't, I wouldn't help you," the landlady said. "I can't see any harm in them staying as planned." She smiled. "It would be one in the eye for your Perky chap, wouldn't it?"

"It certainly would!" Mandy exclaimed. "You're terrific, Mrs Torrance. We weren't expecting such leniency!"

Leigh was frowning. "It might prove embarrassing for the girls," he said doubtfully.

"It need not be," Mrs Torrance told him. "I have another room I can fix up as a sitting-room and there is an adjoining room. It's nearer the bathroom, too, on the second floor. The girls are on the top floor near the kitchen. They don't have to see the men if they arrange when to use the stove."

Audrey nodded her head approvingly. "It seems a good idea. I can move back into my room then."

"There will be some shifting of furniture to be done!" her landlady warned her.

"We can all help with that," Mandy said.

"What about rent?" Leigh asked worriedly.

"We can discuss that later. It won't cost you a fortune. I think we ought to get them sorted out first. They must be a little worried themselves."

Leigh sighed with relief. "You have taken a load off my back. It's extremely good of you! The girls are lucky to have such a kind and generous landlady."

"I reap some benefit, too," she said complacently. "The girls are good company. I enjoy having them here. They tell me what happens at the hospital and sometimes I feel part of their daily life. This house would feel pretty empty with only Blackie and me in it!"

The cat purred and buried its head in her lap but she shooed it off. "Come on then! There's no time like the present. Shall we make a start?"

After they had explained the position to the New Zealanders, things went with a swing. The visitors threw themselves into the spirit of moving the rooms around. Mrs Torrance was glad of their strength.

"It's twice as quick when you have a man to help you," she stated with satisfaction.

As Mandy and Audrey had rearranged a couple of the rooms once before, they heartily agreed. Also it was great fun having three men to order about.

When they had finished, it seemed that the two visitors were going to be very comfortable indeed. They were a good-natured pair and Audrey for one felt quite taken with them.

They rounded the evening off with toast, baked beans and coffee eaten in the landlady's kitchen. And by that time all were on the best of terms. Even Dr Guthrie had forgotten his previous anxieties.

"Sorry, I couldn't muster anything else," Mrs Torrance remarked. "I wasn't expecting to have company. Not five of you! It's a wonder I had enough bread."

"You have been absolutely wonderful!" Mandy exclaimed before she left. "Audrey and I will make it up to you . . . I promise!"

"I know you will." The woman's lined face creased into a smile. "Be off with you now. I've had enough for one day."

Leigh grabbed Mandy's arm as she passed him in the small hall. He kept her there by his side until the others had gone up the stairs.

"I wanted to thank you," he said gruffly. "I couldn't say anything in front of the others."

"I'm thankful it has turned out so well," she replied.

They were so close that Leigh only had to bend his head to press a kiss on her soft smiling lips. Mandy's green eyes revealed the shock his unexpected caress had given her. Until now he had always kept his distance.

Leigh moved away from her when Audrey called out.

"Keep in touch," he said quietly. "I can't stay now. I'm due back at the hospital."

"Mandy! Where are you?" Audrey shouted once again.

"Coming!" she replied as she ascended the stairs.

She felt very strange . . . disorientated in fact . . . as she proceeded very slowly to the third floor. She had expected Leigh to be pleased but not to the extent of embracing her. He must have got carried away, she thought. In the ward this afternoon I didn't exist for him. He was too involved with Sister Blake.

Audrey was looking agitated. "Where have you been?" she exclaimed. "I'm feeling all at sixes and sevens! I need you to talk to."

"They didn't move your bed back into your room," Mandy remarked as they entered her bedroom. "Shall we leave it as it is for tonight? I'm feeling exhausted!"

"Yes. We might as well. We've got heaps to talk about."

Mandy did not feel in the mood for chatting. She did try to keep the conversation going although at times it caused her considerable effort. Her mind would keep floating back to that moment in the hall when Leigh had forgotten to be precise and clinical.

"Which one did you like best?" Audrey asked as she sat on her bed hugging her knees.

"They both seemed pleasant," Mandy replied absent-mindedly.

"I preferred Leslie. He's the big blond one in case you have forgotten."

"I remember quite well! He's the one I saw first."

"Perky's secret is out now," Audrey said in satisfied tones. "I wonder what they make of his behaviour?"

"There's no need to gloat! I'm sure they were amused more than anything.

I expect they weren't all that surprised. But they were too polite to mention their doubts."

"Our landlady took to them," Audrey remarked cheerfully.

"That was just as well," Mandy said flatly. "She came up trumps. I think she behaved better than any of us."

"I know what you mean! I felt bad, too. I hated deceiving her," Audrey said seriously.

Mandy smiled. "She will forgive us. I'm feeling more concerned about Dr Guthrie."

"Why do you have to worry about him?"

"He has got to face his boss. I wonder what they will say to one another? Will Dr Perkins ignore his mistake?"

Audrey said truculently, "Leigh ought to demand an explanation."

"He won't dare do that!" Mandy exclaimed. "It's so unfair! I'm sure Perkins knew before they came that he had interpreted the communication wrongly."

"If he did, he had a nerve bringing them here!"

Mandy chuckled. "To give the devil his due, he did come with them to see what the accommodation was like. Obviously he was satisfied. He hasn't complained to anyone."

"If he had," Audrey said indignantly, "I would have told him a few home truths!"

"You have only to open the door to realise the house is comfortable and clean. Everything shines and smells fresh. Dr Perkins wouldn't bother too much about our reaction," Mandy said.

"He ought to! We ought to have been his first concern. After all we did go to a lot of trouble for him."

"I doubt whether Leigh told him that much," Mandy replied with a yawn.

Audrey frowned. "It seems to me that we aren't getting much credit for what we are putting up with."

"I'm sure Leigh appreciates it."

"Do you think Dr Perkins would have taken his guests away if he hadn't approved of the house?"

"I'm sure he wouldn't have left them here. Dr Perkins may have been playing a little joke on Leigh but he wouldn't damage his own image by causing his visitors discomfort."

"Yes. That makes sense." Audrey nodded her head thoughtfully. "I guess he's not as black as he's painted. I bet Leigh exaggerated."

Mandy was instantly on the defensive. "It can't be easy having to work with a man like that!"

"Okay! I'm not attacking your precious doctor. I'm sure Leigh knows how to look after himself. But he does appear to have a tendency to laden other people with his burdens."

"You make him sound awful." Mandy was looking upset. "You forget. I offered to help him."

"Sorry! I spoke out of turn. I might be able to understand him more if he unbent a little. He never seems to be

137

able to forget his own importance."

Mandy smiled to herself. He did tonight . . . she mused. He went out of his way to thank me . . . in a very sweet way, too! It gave me a wonderful lift and restored my confidence in myself. More so because he acted so spontaneously. It was a pity that Audrey interrupted us. I wasn't able to show him that I cared. She sighed. Now he won't realise how much it meant to me. I wish I could feel sure of him. I like him a lot. But there is a question mark . . . His relationship with Sister Blake warns me to be cautious. I don't want to appear foolish . . .

"Who are you dreaming about now?" Audrey complained. "Don't answer! I know it already. You will have to make the first move in that quarter, my pretty one. He's a career man if ever I saw one!"

"Yes. I'm sure you are right." Mandy yawned pretending that her friend's jibes had gone unnoticed. "I'm going to bed. I'm on early turn tomorrow."

Meanwhile Dr Guthrie was having a rather heated conversation with Dr Perkins. Leigh was incensed at the unfeeling and calculating way his boss had involved him in an embarrassing and upsetting situation. He had felt extremely foolish when he was forced to explain the position to the two New Zealanders. Without damaging his boss's reputation too much, of course!

Fortunately, they had taken it as a genuine mistake. They had realised that their names were to blame. It had happened to them before. Neither of them had met Dr Perkins personally although they had attended his lectures. So it could have been a natural mistake.

"Why didn't the guy tell us himself?" Leslie Davis had asked in slight bewilderment.

Why indeed! Leigh thought now as he faced Dr Perkins who was unconcernedly reading a pamphlet that had been placed on his desk.

Knowing from past experiences that

his boss was only pretending that he was not listening, Leigh battled on:

"As I said, sir. It has all been most embarrassing for the two nurses and myself. Perhaps if you had allowed us to see the correspondence we might have deduced they would be male doctors."

Dr Perkins raised his head. "Are you trying to discredit me, Guthrie?" he asked in ironic tones. "If you are, you are failing dismally. Your attempt is farcical! You have worked yourself into a state over a trifle. For heaven's sake man, pull yourself together! Remember where you are and to whom you are talking!"

Leigh's face whitened with anger. "I'm aware of both, sir," he replied shortly.

"That's a step in the right direction then." Dr Perkins gazed at him thoughtfully. "I did take the trouble to go to the boarding house. I saw for myself that the visitors would be well looked after. That is the end of the matter as far as I'm concerned. When I give my subordinates a task to perform I expect a certain amount of efficiency. Without having to listen to unwarranted complaints, I hasten to add," he said sardonically.

Leigh stood his ground. "The nurses were caused considerable annoyance and inconvenience. One of them had to give up her room."

"If you cast your mind back, Guthrie you will note that I had nothing to do with your arrangement with the nurses. That was your idea, was it not?"

"Yes, sir. I was grateful for their assistance."

Dr Perkins frowned. "I can see no reason for complaint. I telephoned Mrs Torrance a short time ago. She assured me she is willing to have the two men as boarders. At no inconvenience to the two nurses! That sounds very satisfactory." He smiled thinly. "I have to admit, Guthrie that you are more resourceful than I gave you credit for. But you became just a little over zealous. You placed no trust in me! For that I find it difficult to exonerate you. You ought to have known that I would have found quarters for them if they had wished to move."

That was a complete waste of time, Leigh told himself in disgust when he had left the consulting room. He's too righteous to be true! He smiled ruefully. He actually handed out a compliment . . . a back-handed one and rather lukewarm. But it did reveal that he had noticed my efforts. How did I ever get into this? I was warned about Perkins but I didn't think it would be as bad as this! Why didn't I choose another hospital?

I wouldn't have met Mandy if I had done that, he mused smiling faintly. That makes it worth putting up with, I suppose. There's another drawback, too! It's a pity Irene has to be in the picture. Why doesn't she let sleeping dogs lie?

Leigh's outburst had upset him and he went along to his own small surgery to relax and think things over. He knew that it would be hopeless to continue with his work until he was in a quieter frame of mind.

Irene Blake was foremost in his mind as he sat down at his desk. One thing's for sure, he told himself firmly. I'm not going to allow her to interfere with my friendship with Mandy. I finished with all the bitterness and resentment long ago. Why can't Irene do the same? She's an admirable Sister . . . very compassionate . . . but not where I'm concerned! He smiled wryly. It's not only the patients that have problems. Doctors need a shoulder to lean on also . . . only we never allow ourselves that privilege.

A few days later, Leigh called in on Mrs Torrance to see how things were going. He had been fully occupied with Dr Perkins' demands and had had to leave the visitors to their own devices.

He felt reluctant to ask either of the nurses what had been happening. Audrey made him feel uncomfortable.

And Mandy, he felt sure, would not complain if the two men were upsetting her in any way. So the landlady was the best person to ask. She would not hesitate to tell him the truth.

He was sipping a cup of tea when he mentioned the subject of rent. It had been worrying him considerably for Dr Perkins had not offered to pay for his guests.

"Bless you, don't worry about that!" Mrs Torrance exclaimed. "It's all been settled with Leslie and Vivien . . . strange name to give a boy . . . don't you think?"

"I believe it's spelt differently for a girl," Leigh said with a faint smile.

"Well, as I was saying, it's all been sorted out satisfactorily. They have been quite generous and laughed when I said it was too much."

Leigh looked genuinely surprised. "That's good news! I was going to see to it for them."

"If I were you, Dr Guthrie, I wouldn't broach the subject. I think they might take offence. From what I gathered, they were expecting to pay their share."

"Dr Perkins didn't give me that impression."

Mrs Torrance said seriously, "I wouldn't take too much notice of what that man says. Throw in a pinch of salt and you might get at the truth. Have another scone, Doctor!"

"No, thanks! I've had three already." Leigh laughed. "I shall be falling asleep in surgery. I have some patients to see when I get back."

"Pity the girls aren't here. The boys are taking them out tonight. They are going to a theatre in the West End."

"It sounds as if they are all getting along well," Leigh remarked.

"That's not difficult. They are a friendly pair. Leslie seems keen on Mandy. I sense that it doesn't go down too well with Audrey. She's usually paired off with Vivien. He's the quieter of the two."

Leigh endeavoured to keep his voice

unconcerned as he asked, "Has Mandy got a preference?"

"I wouldn't know. She's deeper than Audrey who readily shows her feelings. Mandy is more thoughtful. She always has an excuse for others' mistakes and never pushes herself. She has had a good family life, I would say."

Leigh smiled. "I shall have to watch how I behave, Mrs Torrance. You are a close observer and give a shrewd summing up."

The woman chuckled. "You make me sound like a judge. I've lived longer than you have. That's all there is to it."

The two nurses arrived home just as Leigh opened the front door to go out. They both stared at him in surprise.

"Why didn't you tell us you were coming?" Audrey exclaimed in some dismay. "We're going out and have to rush off to change."

He smiled across at Mandy. "I know. Don't worry. I'm on my way back to the hospital. Have a good time!"

Mandy hid her disappointment and smiled back. She had not seen him for days. He would have to come this evening when she was unable to see him!

"I don't think he wanted to see us," Audrey said shrewdly when they had gained the top landing. "He would have telephoned us if he had wanted any information."

"It did look that way," Mandy said flatly. "He doesn't seem very friendly, does he?"

"What did you expect? He only wanted your assistance. Don't break your heart over him. He's only another — "

"Don't say it!" Mandy shut her up before she could finish. "I don't care what you think! I like him. I expect he's got a good reason for not coming round here."

"I can guess what it is, too," Audrey retorted. "Sister Blake could soon disillusion you. Keep your eyes on her. There has been something going on between her and Leigh. It's rather

147

puzzling because it's more of a hate relationship."

"I've noticed," Mandy told her. Then changing the subject rapidly she went on, "Do hurry up! We've only got half an hour to get ready. See you later!"

Mandy breathed a sigh of relief when she entered her room and closed the door. Sometimes Audrey's bluntness was too much for her to take. Especially when it concerned Leigh. The mention of Sister Blake was a bitter pill to swallow for it confirmed her own fears. The fears which she had kidded herself were imaginary.

I can't start digging up Leigh's past without arousing suspicion, she told herself resignedly. I don't know any of the older nurses well enough. Yet I expect they were acquainted with Leigh and Irene Blake before he went away. Sister North would have told me . . . and Tony Southwood knew both of them. He would tell me . . .

She shrank away from the idea of

pumping Tony about Leigh. Most likely he would blurt it out to others and what a fool she would feel then. Leigh wouldn't be over the moon about it either!

I expect it will solve itself eventually, she told herself not very convincingly. He's not rushing to date me so there's no need for me to unravel the mystery. Anyway it's not my concern. I might stir up more than I bargained for!

Hurriedly she prepared herself for the evening out. She had not been looking forward to it overmuch. But her mood changed when they were in the taxi speeding towards Shaftesbury Avenue. Leslie and Vivien were good company. It was evident that they were enjoying themselves. It would have been difficult not to have taken advantage of their good humour.

The only disturbing factor was Audrey's undisguised desire for Leslie's company. Not caring one way or the other, Mandy did try to switch partners. But Leslie was too astute for her. When

Mandy changed places with Audrey in the theatre, the men did likewise. So Audrey found Vivien remaining at her side.

"I'm sorry, Audrey," Mandy whispered as soon as she found the opportunity during the interval. "I did my best."

The one fear Mandy had was that Leslie might become serious about her. So far she had seen no signs of it but she could not rid herself of the possibility. Audrey sensed and feared it also. She was swift to put Mandy on her guard.

"It wouldn't be fair to encourage him," she said seriously. "We both know you aren't fancy free."

Mandy smiled reassuringly. "I'm not attracted to him," she said. "He's good company, that's all."

A few days had elapsed since their outing but Audrey would keep mentioning it. Mandy had been on the early shift and was enjoying a few quiet minutes before she began to get ready to go out. But Audrey had burst in on her so she sat down resignedly to listen.

Audrey was saying, "Leslie more or less ignores me . . . I can't think why! Vivien seems impressed and enjoys my company."

"Perhaps that is why Leslie is cool," Mandy said.

Audrey's eyes widened. "You think Leslie is acting that way because he knows Vivien likes me?"

"It's possible, isn't it? They may have come to some arrangement."

"Why didn't they arrange it the other way!" Audrey exclaimed irritably. "I'm sure that's the truth of it. Only Vivien is hanging on to me to give Leslie a chance with you."

Mandy chuckled. "You pessimist! He's not being very successful with me." She broke off and gazed at her friend thoughtfully. "There is a way we could resolve it."

"I can't see how, short of being rude to them!" Audrey said gloomily.

"You could tell Vivien that I'm

secretly engaged to someone I've known a long time."

Audrey's eyes brightened. "At least they would know that you aren't free. It might work."

Mandy asked doubtfully, "Are you sure you want to find out?"

"I would know then if Leslie was interested in you. It would be more definite," Audrey said.

"I wouldn't count on it! Neither of them might bother to lift an eyebrow."

Both girls glanced at each other and laughed.

"I think it's worth trying," Audrey said seriously. "It will anchor you and let me free. It's only fair to let them know. If either of them are serious I will soon find out."

"Now you are being an optimist!" Mandy grinned. "I thought you were intent on a career!"

"I am. This doesn't alter anything," Audrey said defensively.

"Who are you kidding? You are head over heels in love with Leslie! You have all the signs. I've never known you to be so agitated over trifles," Mandy teased.

Audrey looked troubled. "I can't forget he's only here for a vacation. Perhaps I ought to have nothing more to do with him."

"That would be the sensible way to deal with it. Could you be brave enough to do that? It would be painful."

"Not at the moment!"

"It's hopeless then," Mandy said. "It will be much worse later on."

"I'm afraid it's too late now. It's happened. I can't just destroy the feeling I have for him! It's there for good."

"You advised me to forget Leigh," Mandy reminded her.

Audrey smiled ruefully. "I didn't understand what it was like."

"We seem to be in the same boat," Mandy said sadly. "You have more of a chance to succeed than I have."

"The trouble is that I haven't too

long to prove that," Audrey replied unhappily.

Mandy who had been looking very thoughtful said, "It's a pity we can't tell Mrs Torrance about my phoney engagement. But I really couldn't deceive her again."

"It would sound more authentic coming from her. She would be bound to tell the men. Why don't we tell her the truth?"

"No. She likes the New Zealanders. She wouldn't understand our predicament," Mandy said. "You will have to drop it casually into the conversation."

"Very well. It wouldn't sound right coming from you. I will mention it tonight," Audrey said. "What time did they tell us to be ready?"

"Eight o'clock!" Mandy glanced at her fob watch and jumped to her feet. "It's nearly that now!"

"Relax! We are only going for a drink. They want to visit a real pub. I thought we would take them to the Lamb." Audrey chuckled. "That sounds appropriate, doesn't it?"

"In more ways than one!" Mandy could not hide her anxiety. "You realise that some of the hospital staff go there? We will have a spot-light on us and life will be difficult tomorrow. Can you deal with that?"

"I can't see why not. It won't be the first time," Audrey said bluntly. "It will give them something to talk about. Our nursing pals will be green with envy when they see us with Leslie and Vivien. I will be able to endure the jeers quite easily!"

6

THE Lamb was crowded. Lights blazed outside flooding the forecourt. Inside there was subdued lighting and soft music. Mandy and Audrey were able to order snacks at the bar whilst the men chose the drinks. Then they were fortunate enough to find seats at a table tucked at the back, well away from the bar.

"We can see and not be bothered here," Audrey explained to the two men who were looking delighted. "You said you wanted to savour the real thing."

"It's terrific! The atmosphere is great!" Leslie exclaimed. "I guessed it would be something like this. My father used to rave about your inns and public houses. We try to copy them but there's something missing."

"Old Father Time," Mandy said smilingly.

Vivien nodded. "We have bars but nothing like this! The outside is very misleading. I expected a grimy, shabby interior."

"Most of them are pretty good these days. They have had a face lift," Mandy told him. "Occasionally you come across an ancient one. But usually the food is reliable."

"People still smoke a lot over here," Leslie remarked. "Don't you do anything about it?"

"There are government warnings. It has been cut down considerably. Don't forget we have a huge population!" Audrey said.

Mandy was not paying much attention to the conversation. Her eyes were focused on two doctors who had come in together. One was Tony, the other Leigh Guthrie. She held her breath as he glanced about him. Evidently he had not noticed them for he did not come over.

"Do you come here frequently?" Leslie smilingly repeated his question aware that Mandy's mind had strayed.

She pulled herself together quickly. "No, not often. Our nursing officers don't approve of their staff coming here. That makes it difficult for us because a lot of the hospital people use it."

"I hope we aren't going to get you into hot water!"

"That's why we chose this table," Mandy said. "I don't think we have been seen."

She kept quiet about Dr Guthrie, not wishing to draw Audrey's attention to him. He appeared to be interested in someone sitting at a table on the other side of the bar. She saw him say a few words to Tony before he picked up his drink and edged his way round the corner of the bar.

Very intrigued by now, Mandy moved her chair slightly so that she could see more easily. She was not sure at first which table he was making for. But when he pulled a chair out and sat down, Mandy realised with a pang of dismay that the woman he had joined was none other than Sister Blake!

Mandy had rarely seen her out of uniform. Tonight she was looking quite breathtaking with her dark hair falling loosely to her shoulders. She had taken off her jacket revealing the soft frills of her white blouse at the neck and cuffs. Perhaps it's the light, Mandy thought. She looks years younger. How lovely she is!

If she had been sitting closer, she would have seen that charming expression change to one of distaste when Leigh appeared at the table. Mandy could only see their actions. Leigh leaned across the table and held out his hand. It appeared to be a gesture of appeasement for he held it there for some time.

Obviously it was to no avail. Mandy had to bite back her gasp of astonishment when Sister reacted so violently to this peace offering. Picking up her handbag, Irene gave Leigh's outstretched hand such a terrific blow that she nearly fell sideways off her chair. She reseated herself immediately and sat in stony silence as Leigh recovered from the unexpected shock.

Mandy was unable to observe their faces clearly. All their actions spoke of anger, especially Irene's. She was not disguising her contempt! Her defiance was puzzling. Mandy had always considered her as calm, efficient and self-controlled; a Sister who tempered justice with mercy. This was a different woman, one Mandy had not seen before.

She glanced quickly at her companions but they were deep in conversation. This gave her a chance to keep her attention on the pair who appeared by now to be having a silent battle.

It did not last long. Dr Guthrie had evidently had enough. He pushed his glass to the middle of the table, rose to his feet and walked out. He had to pass much closer to Mandy's table this time before he could gain the exit. His face was pale and drawn, his lips tightly compressed. But he held himself with dignity. It was apparent that he saw no one other than those in his direct path.

"You are very quiet, Mandy!" Leslie was smiling at her indulgently. "Have you been dreaming of your secret young man."

She frowned and looked at Audrey who slightly nodded her head.

"Don't look so troubled. We can be discreet," Vivien told her. "You haven't heard a word that has been said. I can guess from your expression."

Mandy was quick to defend herself. "It's warm in here. I feel rather sleepy."

"Audrey said you wouldn't mind us knowing," Vivien said.

Mandy smiled. "You won't be here that long, will you?"

"Long enough to become fond of both of you," Leslie said. His blue eyes twinkled. "I'm not surprised about you. Neither of you look the type to remain single for long."

"Thank you! I suppose that's meant

to be a compliment." Mandy said. "But we are both interested in what we do. It wouldn't break our hearts to remain single a little longer."

Audrey interrupted quickly, "You two are dark horses! Are you both married?"

The men chuckled. "We wouldn't be over here enjoying ourselves if we were! Our wives would have something to say about that!"

The girls were intuitive enough not to ask any more personal questions and the evening passed amicably. It had been an enlightening one for Mandy. She realised now that to go on centring her thoughts on Leigh would be disastrous. She would have to relinquish all ties with him. Not that she had many she was thankful to own! They were acquaintances, that was all. The thought gave her no joy. Sadly she reflected that she had only herself to blame for being too imaginative and hopeful.

The nurses contrived successfully to

have lunch together the next day. Mandy was not as eager as Audrey was to go over the events of the previous evening. And she was relieved that her companions had not seen the disquieting conflict between Leigh and Sister Blake. It would have been very difficult to explain!

"Do you feel any wiser, Audrey?" Mandy asked after they had transferred their lunches from the trays to the table.

Audrey looked disgusted as she sat down and set out the knives and forks. "I feel annoyed I mentioned your phoney engagement. Neither of them turned a hair. And I didn't see any signs of a change of attitude. Leslie still remained glued to you!"

"I did warn you!" Mandy smiled. "It's early days yet. Give it time to sink in."

"I thought at least one of them would look disappointed," Audrey said truculently.

Mandy frowned. "They might be

pleased. They may have girl friends back home."

"It's beginning to look like that," Audrey replied unhappily. "They just wanted some feminine company."

"You can't blame them," Mandy said. "They have behaved exceptionally well."

"I know." Audrey sighed resignedly. "I have to get back to reality and stop all this wishful thinking."

"Don't lose heart, Audrey," Mandy said sympathetically. "It happens to most of us at some time. Perhaps it's good for our characters!"

Audrey chuckled. "That's a unique way of looking at it!"

When Audrey left her to return to the ward, Mandy remained at the table musing over what had happened that morning.

There had been the usual rush to get to the hospital on time. Neither Mandy nor Audrey felt very bright after their late night.

It was strange to see Sister Blake

there on the ward giving instructions to her nurses in that cool, no nonsense voice she reserved for the juniors. Afterwards there was the smile that never failed to soften the harshness. This morning, however, Mandy noticed an unusual edge to her voice and her smile seemed forced.

She is still upset over what happened last night, she thought uneasily. What will happen if Dr Guthrie comes to the ward today?

"What's the matter with Sister?" Audrey murmured before she departed to the sluice room. She was to do half an hour there then find a junior to assist her with back-rubbing. It was an active task that had to be enacted a good deal on a medical ward. "She seemed to take great delight in dishing out all the most energetic jobs. They didn't have to be done this morning!"

Mandy whispered back worriedly, "She hasn't given me anything."

"I would disappear if I were you.

She's saving something horrible for you to do; probably bed-scrubbing!"

Staff Nurse was hovering. "Weren't you briefed, Greenwood?" she inquired cheerfully. "Sister was in a hurry this morning. She has to attend a staff meeting. I expect she will be absent all morning. That doesn't mean you can relax. Come with me!"

Assigned to the side wards, Mandy was soon engrossed with checking pulse rates, taking temperatures, adjusting drips and giving injections. The patients were more seriously ill than those on the main ward and Staff Nurse was relieved to have some capable help.

"Diets to see to next," she said crisply. "At this rate we will be finished before the rounds start."

It was always a race against time as Mandy well knew. Behind two screened beds in one of the units, nurses were disinfecting the iron bedsteads. There was a strong smell of lysol when Mandy looked in on them.

"Nearly finished?" she inquired. "Staff wants it all cleared away before the consultants arrive."

The nurses groaned as they straightened up. One of them complained with annoyance.

"She doesn't want much does she? Sister got mixed up this morning. We usually do these jobs later on in the day. I've been told off for starting them before the rounds. We've only got halfway!"

"Things are rather chaotic. Leave it and go back to it later," Mandy advised them. "Don't forget to make yourselves presentable!"

Audrey nearly ran her down with the drinks trolley. She was doing the elevenses and urging the patients to gulp their quota down quickly.

"You are getting around!" Mandy ejaculated. "I always know when Sister is away. You lose all sense of decorum."

Audrey leaned against the trolley and grinned. "The patients enjoy it. We are half an hour ahead! Too much spit and polish takes the joy out of life."

"The juniors who have just tidied the ward would agree with you," Mandy said with a light laugh. "They will have to do it again before the next visitors arrive."

"I'm so glad you see my point!" Audrey commented airily before she sped on her way.

Dr Perkins was due on the ward any minute. Staff Nurse was looking slightly uneasy for she would have to take Sister's place. Mandy kept glancing at her own fob watch. She was eagerly awaiting the arrival of the doctors. Dr Perkins rarely came without four students and three of the medical staff in tow.

I used to wonder why they needed so many on a medical ward, Mandy mused. Now I can understand. It's as busy and nearly as complicated as a surgical ward. Perhaps the patients don't have so much bedside attention . . . many of them can get to the bathroom without assistance . . . but there is plenty to do all the same! I hope the diets aren't changed too much today. Staff and I have got them all sorted out.

She was attempting to make the flowers on the centre table look more interesting when a rush of cool air heralded the consultant and his followers. Staff Nurse lost her cool manner and greeted the great man with warmth. He frowned, slightly raising his bushy eyebrows at her effusive welcome. Mandy felt a little sorry for her. Dr Perkins did have that effect on the less confident nurses. Sister Blake ignored his attempts to undermine her poise. But she had been a sister for a number of years.

Having been given her instructions in advance, Mandy followed at the rear of the cortege. Leigh winked at her as he passed. She smiled an acknowledgement and at the next halt at a bedside, he managed to drop behind also.

"How are you, Mandy? I haven't

seen you lately," he remarked quietly.

"I've been here most days," she replied formally.

She could see scarcely any difference in him. Perhaps his slate-grey eyes were a little more wistful. But then he would be feeling hurt and misjudged! It was surprising that he hadn't found some excuse to avoid the ward.

"Did you know Sister Blake wouldn't be here today?" she asked bravely, suppressing her misgivings.

"No!" He looked rather astonished at her question but swiftly recovered. "Why did you ask me that?" he inquired curiously.

"It was just an idle remark," she replied carelessly.

"I see. It doesn't make much difference. Sister or Staff Nurse can answer our questions and take instructions."

"Yes, of course! It was stupid of me," Mandy said.

He looked amused. "I would never say that of you. Tell me, how are you getting on with the visitors? Have you had much to do with them?"

She nodded and began to walk forward in an attempt to catch up with the group who had gone on ahead. "Audrey and I see them most evenings," she said.

Leigh glanced at his boss, saw that he was not required to give an opinion and went on talking to Mandy.

"As often as that!" he hesitated then added diffidently, "Mrs Torrance said you paired off with Leslie."

Her green eyes became wary. "I suppose that's true. We do seem to get on well together."

"How fortunate for him!" he said dryly.

Mandy glanced at him nervously, surprised at his snappy reply. After all, he was the one who had turned the New Zealanders over to the nurses instead of looking after them himself. He didn't appear to be at all grateful! Quite the reverse in fact!

"From what you said I thought we

were expected to entertain them," she said flatly.

He caught her hand but she pulled it away. He had a lot of explaining to do before she would allow him any privileges. She was still recovering from the shock of the previous evening. Also it was strange that he had never mentioned Sister Blake to her.

Leigh was looking troubled. "Don't take offence, Mandy. Not you of all people! Confound it! I never appear right in your eyes, do I?"

She could not endure the hurt in his eyes. With heightened colour in her cheeks, she dashed after Dr Perkins and his followers who were disappearing into the inner corridor.

At the door she turned back to whisper loud enough for Leigh to hear, "They are going to the side wards. Hurry! We will get into trouble."

After that all chance of a private conversation faded. Dr Perkins demanded Leigh's presence at a bedside and the ranks closed in about them. Staff Nurse whisked Mandy off to a patient the doctor had dealt with and left her there in the single unit.

"You are to remain here until I send you a relief. She has to be closely watched. She has been sedated but alert me if she shows any sign at all!"

For half an hour Mandy was kept busy. Pulse rate and temperature had to be taken at frequent intervals. Charts had to be filled in and visitors kept at bay. Mandy was beginning to run out of excuses to give to the anxious relatives when Staff Nurse appeared again.

"What are all these people doing here!" she demanded sharply. "She's not allowed visitors. Surely your common sense told you that?"

"I haven't allowed any of them in the unit," Mandy said defensively smarting under the sting of her senior's voice. It definitely was not her day! What was the matter with everybody?

"Get rid of them, Greenwood! Then

you can go to lunch. When you return report to Sister."

Mandy's heart sank. The last person she felt like seeing was Irene Blake. Why couldn't Staff have given her something to keep her occupied for most of the afternoon? Mandy sensed that Sister Blake would still be feeling irritable and she was proved right. Irene was in a mood all day and the nurses heaved a sigh of relief when it was time to leave.

"What a day!" Audrey exclaimed as she and Mandy walked home together. "I can't understand why Sister was in such a foul mood. She was positively sadistic! If it goes on I shall be asking for a transfer!"

"She did seem to be in a temper," Mandy agreed.

"Whatever the cause she needn't have lashed out at us," Audrey complained. "I was scared she was going to keep us late. I want to wash my hair."

Mandy glanced at her shining brown curls and smiled. "It looks all right to me. You are lucky having curly hair."

"I would rather have a few waves like you!"

Mandy chuckled. "Nobody likes their own hair. What are we doing tonight?"

"Nothing, absolutely nothing! Isn't it wonderful?" Audrey cried. "Leslie and Vivien went to the country to visit some relatives today. Didn't they tell you?"

"If they did I didn't take it in," Mandy replied. "How very nice! We can really relax, rest our feet and spend the evening in the bath if we want to."

"The men are bound to come back late so we can have an early night," Audrey said. "I will tell Mrs Torrance and put a note in the hall. Then we won't be disturbed."

Mandy laughed. "You aren't taking any chances!"

"They are on holiday. They tend to forget that we have done a day's work before they take us out." Audrey grinned. "They *would* have to be more energetic than most men we know!"

The weather had been warm and sunny but the nurses had had little chance to get out and enjoy it. Thursday was Mandy's half day so she planned to forget about all the small jobs that needed doing and go to the park. The river was close by and she loved watching the barges and river boats chug through the sparkling waters. She would be able to sit under the spreading branches of the trees and let the warmth from the dappled sunlight soak right into her.

She left the hospital at twelve, had a bite to eat with Mrs Torrance then went up to her room to change. When she emerged she was as casually dressed as any young woman with time on her hands. Blue jeans, an open-necked shirt blouse and a tiny blue waistcoat all served to highlight her slim figure and copper-gold hair. Outside in the street, she slung her bag over her shoulder and started to walk.

She had only gone a few yards when a familiar voice hailed her.

"Mandy! Wait for me!"

She swung round, her green eyes wide with astonishment.

"What are you doing here at this time of the day?" she inquired with a faint smile.

Leigh said breathlessly, "I thought I was going to miss you. I passed you in my car. I tried to attract your attention. I had to park the car quickly and run after you."

"I wasn't expecting to see anyone I knew."

"I gathered that! Where are you off to?"

Mandy hesitated and glanced at him doubtfully. "I was going for a walk in the park."

"Good! I will drive you there." Leigh grasped her arm and steered her in the opposite direction. "I had to park on the main road, hence the rush. Sorry about that!"

"Aren't you supposed to be working?"

"I've taken a couple of hours off."

Mandy smiled at his boyish smile. The formidable, aloof expression that so often daunted her in the hospital had vanished. He looked so much happier and relaxed.

Mandy's green eyes danced. "What a coincidence you passed just at the right moment!" she teased.

He grinned. "Yes, wasn't it? I happened to meet Audrey. She told me you had a free afternoon."

"I feel flattered. You would have been a great help if I had decided on a shopping spree. You could have carried the parcels!"

"You wouldn't do that to me, would you?"

Mandy shrugged her slender shoulders. "There's no problem. It's fortunate for you that I decided on the park."

There were few people about as they strolled along the tow path. One or two senior citizens were occupying the benches and bored young women were chasing their energetic toddlers.

"Do you feel slightly out of place here?" Leigh asked amusedly.

"A little," Mandy replied. "I know what you mean."

Leigh stooped to retrieve a youngster's red ball. He tossed it back and received a grateful smile from the harassed mother.

"I find it much the same wherever I go," he said. "The unsocial hours plunge us into different worlds."

Mandy nodded. "Free afternoons are solitary ones usually."

Leigh frowned. "I wish I could stay the entire afternoon."

"Do you ever get out of London for a break?" Mandy asked carelessly.

"It's strange you should ask that! I was thinking only the other day that I ought to go home soon. My parents live in Dorset. They are very understanding and welcome me anytime even if the visit is brief."

"Do you take your friends with you sometimes?"

"Occasionally but my colleagues

rarely have the same time free as I do."

"That's a pity," Mandy said. "I really meant do you take your girl friends there?"

"No!" He grinned with amusement. "I've never committed myself that much."

"I find that difficult to believe." Mandy gave him a curious glance.

He said seriously, "Why? Have I got a reputation?"

"The grape-vine couples you with Sister Blake. Didn't you want to take her to see your parents?"

"No! Certainly not!" he exclaimed vehemently.

The suddenness of the change in him shook Mandy so much that she was unable to move. Her entire being was filled with dismay as she realised the damage she had done. Leigh looked so frightening with his shoulders squared as if to do battle. The hardened jaw and steely glint in his eyes sent shivers running through her. She had never seen him so angry! She felt lost and bewildered as she confronted his alien figure.

"Has Irene been talking to you?" he demanded as he grasped her roughly by the wrist.

"Of course not! Let me go!" Mandy exclaimed. "You are hurting me!"

His hand fell away and he apologised swiftly. "I'm sorry. The mere mention of that woman makes me see red."

"I can see that," Mandy said. "Would you care to tell me why she upsets you so?"

He shook his head. "It's too complicated."

"Were you engaged to her once?"

His mouth twisted with bitterness. "No way would I marry into that family!"

Mandy glanced at him in bewilderment as they began to walk on along the path. "She is very attractive," she said nervous now after his outburst. But she couldn't just ignore it!

"She is years older than I am." He

took in Mandy's pensive profile and said gently, "That's not the reason. If you were her age it would make no difference." He sighed. "I wish I could tell you more, Mandy. I'm afraid, that's the truth of it. It would be wise for both of us to go our separate ways."

Mandy said unhappily, "That sounds very drastic. I would like to help you."

"Bless you! You have already done that." He glanced swiftly at his wristwatch and frowned. "I will have to leave you. I don't suppose you want to go back yet?"

She shook her head. "It's too sunny. I will stay until it gets cooler."

"Wise girl! By the way, I forgot to tell you. Perkins asked me to thank you and Audrey for your assistance. He said he appreciated what you had done and if ever you needed a favour you weren't to hesitate over asking him."

Mandy burst out laughing. "My

goodness, I never expected that!" she exclaimed.

"He's not as bad as he has been painted," Leigh told her. "I'm getting to know him now. He puts on that omnipotent air but underneath he's very human and vulnerable."

Mandy smiled. "You mean he's like the rest of us!"

And on that amusing comment they parted. Leigh strode towards the main path that would take him to the exit and Mandy sought a pleasant spot where she could sit down and rest.

Sister Blake must have a split personality, she decided as she enjoyed the warm sunshine. The calm efficient appearance she reveals to us in hospital hides an excitable, unreasonable character.

Mandy found it very hard to believe. After all she had worked with Sister for some months and never seen her lose control. If she had not witnessed that violent scene she would have assumed that Leigh was to blame. Perhaps he was, she thought unhappily. No row is one-sided. But Sister must have done something bad to cause him to dislike her so much. I saw him offering an olive branch but she would have none of it.

She sighed heavily. I can't understand either of them! It hurts to think Leigh behaved badly but if he is innocent, what caused Irene to be so angry! I always liked her. The nurses and medical staff respect her. How can I believe she is irrational now?

★ ★ ★

The New Zealanders had not returned from their trip into the country. Their day out had stretched to nearly a week. Mandy wondered if they would be there when she got back. But Audrey's long face told her that the men had not returned.

"Mrs Torrance said that they came back for their gear then went off again," Audrey explained unhappily.

Mandy frowned. "Do you mean for good?"

"I don't know. I hope not!"

"Cheer up! Don't let it upset you," Mandy said consolingly. "They wouldn't go off without saying farewell to us."

Audrey nodded. "They told Mrs Torrance they would be back but that is often said and not meant."

"Perhaps it is for the best," Mandy said. "It has all been very painful for you."

Audrey smiled forlornly. "I would rather have that than not see Leslie again. How am I going to endure another week of it?"

"We both appear to be in the same boat," Mandy reflected sadly. "Why don't we kick over the traces ourselves? We could go out and enjoy a few sprees."

"How could we without male companionship?"

"We have done it before," Mandy smiled. "If you can't bear the thought

185

of doing it alone, phone Reggie. Tony would oblige but we would have to foot the bill."

"Can we afford that?" Audrey asked doubtfully.

"No. It will have to be Reggie or go on our own."

"I will speak to him," Audrey said her expression brightening. "He gave me his number before he left."

Reggie was out but the man who answered the call said he would pass on the message. And an hour later Reggie telephoned sounding quite jubilant.

"Why haven't you got in touch before?" he inquired. "You know you can rely on me. Where do you want to go? There are two of you? Okay, I can soon fix that."

"You don't have to," Audrey said. "Don't get any ideas. We feel like a little entertainment. We have to be back before twelve o'clock."

"When haven't you been able to rely on me?" he asked in hurt tones. "We will call for you at seven-thirty and

186

get you back before midnight. How's that?"

"Do you mean this evening?" Audrey asked dazedly.

"Sure, why not? I'm free. I might not get another opportunity this week."

Audrey glanced inquiringly at Mandy who had been standing by her. She nodded and Audrey returned to her call.

"Okay! We will be ready. Goodbye for now!"

Audrey laughed. "I never expected that! He sounded quite excited."

"He hasn't been at St Jude's very long. Doctors get lonely as well, I expect," Mandy pointed out.

"Yes. I tend to forget that. And Reggie isn't exactly the answer to a maiden's prayer!"

"Don't be unkind! He is going to feed us," Mandy said. "He is too short and rather plain but he is a very nice man. I've always liked him."

"In that case you can have Reggie. I will have the other one," Audrey said.

Mandy looked surprised. "Are you sure? I thought you might feel safer with Reggie. You know him so well."

"It will be good for me. It will put me on my mettle."

Mrs Torrance came from her living-room when she heard them come down the stairs. She lingered to admire their outfits.

"I will say this for you two," she asserted. "You don't mope about feeling sorry for yourselves. I expected a couple of long faces after the news about Leslie and Vivien."

"I expect you miss them, too," Mandy said.

"Yes, I do, very much. But I expect they will be back to spend their last few weeks here. They aren't the sort to disappear without thanking us. I must say you two have done yourselves proud. You look as glamorous as a couple of stage stars!"

Audrey glanced at Mandy and chuckled. "Our escort expects us to look like that. I'm glad you approve.

We thought we had overdone it."

"I hope he takes you somewhere appropriate. It would be a pity to waste the effect!" Mrs Torrance exclaimed.

Mandy laughed. "He will. The expense won't worry him. So we are going to enjoy ourselves."

"Do you both good!" the landlady replied. "There's the bell now. Have a good time!"

"We won't be too late," Mandy told her.

Both girls waved as they hurried along the passage to the door. Mrs Torrance hurriedly brushed away a recalcitrant tear and retreated to her own lonely domain.

7

REGGIE was delighted to have the opportunity to take the two nurses out for the evening. Mandy had always been a special favourite. Apart from admiring her skill as a nurse, he considered her an interesting person. He was not concerned with forming a serious attachment at the moment. His career was too important. So, having the chance of female companionship without strings pleased him considerably.

Audrey discovered that she knew his friend Hugh Turner. She did not dislike him so they made a happy foursome. They went to one of the various clubs that Reggie belonged to where they could dine, watch a cabaret and dance afterwards if they wished to do so.

"It's really great!" Audrey whispered

to Mandy halfway through the delicious dinner.

Mandy smiled and nodded. She also was enjoying herself. At first she had felt rather guilty because they had telephoned Reggie. But after seeing his genuine pleasure at being in their company, she relaxed and revelled in the luxury of an expensive evening's entertainment.

It is just what Audrey and I needed, she thought with a sigh of contentment. We have had quite a few problems lately. This will make us forget for a few hours.

Later on when Hugh took Audrey to gyrate on the tiny dance floor, Mandy was able to ask Reggie about his new post. He was a first rate physician but was too modest to boast about his success.

"It's interesting," he told her with a shy grin. "There's more scope for me to air my own theories. St Adrian's stifled me."

Mandy nodded. "It tends to do that to all of us."

"Don't condemn it too much!" Reggie chided her. "It's a good reliable hospital where a patient can feel safe."

Mandy chuckled. "That isn't possible at your present hospital I suppose? I would think twice about having you experiment on me!"

He looked at her reproachfully. "You know it's not like that! St Adrian's is a wee bit old-fashioned. That's all I meant."

"Did Dr Perkins have something to do with your departure from St Adrian's?" Mandy asked curiously.

Reggie laughed. "He didn't persuade me to stay!" He became serious and glanced at her thoughtfully. "That's enough about me. Tell me about your life."

Mandy smiled faintly. "It's not progressing all that well so there's nothing to tell."

"That's not what I heard!" Reggie exclaimed. "What about the two New Zealanders you and Audrey have been looking after? Are they relatives?"

"No!" Mandy chuckled. "Someone is keeping you up to date with our news! As it happens they are Dr Perkins' protégés. Aren't you thankful you left?"

Reggie frowned. "Are you telling me I would have had them on my hands?"

"It would have been most probable."

"How did you get involved?" he asked curiously.

She smiled. "It's a long story. Briefly . . . the consultant handed them over to Dr Guthrie. He was unable to find accommodation for them so he asked me if I could do something."

"You know Guthrie pretty well then." Reggie was looking slightly puzzled as he went on, "I thought he was tied up with that Ward Sister . . . I've forgotten her name."

"Sister Blake?"

"That's her! Nice-looking woman . . . years older than Guthrie . . . not my taste but then there's no accounting for some people's!"

Mandy said patiently, "At the time I didn't know Dr Guthrie. It was Sister North's suggestion that I might be able to help. She had to let him down at the last minute."

"Yes! I remember now. She went off in a great hurry. I was asked to that party but I couldn't make it. Pity! I would have enjoyed it with you there."

"It's lucky that Audrey and I have an understanding landlady," Mandy remarked. "She agreed to let two rooms to the men."

"I'm surprised at Guthrie! Why did he bother you when he could have asked Irene Blake?"

Mandy hid her astonishment. "Would she have been able to help him?" she asked.

"I would have thought so. She has a large house somewhere, in Chiswick, I think. Perhaps she has sold it. That sister of hers might have had something to do with it. I wonder what happened to her!"

194

"You sound as if you knew Sister Blake well."

Reggie nodded. "Most of my crowd knew her. She was married once. I believe the chap died. There was a lot of gossip at one time about Guthrie and her. She keeps to herself nowadays, I believe."

Mandy frowned. "You are making it more mysterious by the minute. How does the sister come into it?"

"She was a remarkable girl . . . younger than Irene. She was a wild one and no mistake! Strangely beautiful she was and very contrary! Guthrie knew her. That's how we all came to hear of her. She turned up at the hospital on several occasions. Guthrie treated her for some minor illness. I forget now what it was. At the time he was working as a locum for Irene's doctor — " Reggie broke off, meditated for a second or two then exclaimed with a hint of excitement in his voice," Irene was terribly possessive about her sister. The girl must have been seventeen, perhaps eighteen then.

Guthrie was given a bad time. He and Irene used to clash frequently."

They still do! Mandy thought in faint amusement. But tactfully she kept her musing to herself.

"It must have been quite an exciting time," she remarked. "Dr Guthrie and Sister Blake *were* in the limelight!"

"I don't see much of Leigh these days," Reggie said. "I miss the old crowd. We are scattered far and wide now."

"You ought to try to keep in touch," Mandy said carelessly. She was watching Audrey and Hugh who were dancing with evident enjoyment.

Reggie put his glass down so abruptly that he spilt some of the wine. "She was sent off to a mental home!" he ejaculated. "Fancy forgetting that!"

Mandy stared at him in amazement. "Who are you talking about?" she asked curiously.

"Irene's sister! Frances . . . that was her name. She had this breakdown and never recovered. There was some rumour at the time about a broken attachment but I never met the man or heard his name spoken. Sister Blake nearly went to pieces herself."

"Who made the decision to send her to a home?"

"I never knew that. I wasn't that close! I doubt if it was Guthrie." Reggie had lost interest and was grinning across the tables at their two companions. "They are wearing their feet away quite happily. Shall we do likewise?" he asked.

It was a very satisfactory evening, Mandy reflected after they had reached home just before midnight. As well as having a lovely meal and lots of fun, she had learned more about Irene and Leigh. In some ways it had allayed her fear that the two were closer than they pretended.

It wasn't a lovers' quarrel that I witnessed, she decided with infinite relief. I have a suspicion that their connection is something to do with Irene's sister.

Whether it was to her own advantage or not she could not say. But until she knew the entire truth she was not going to allow herself to dwell on what might be. Wishful thinking could cause pain and embarrassment.

An unusual event which occurred the next morning as Mandy was walking to the hospital made her own worries seem trivial in comparison. A woman was knocked down almost in front of her and the car that had hit her did not stop.

It was early, just before six o'clock and there were few people about. It took Mandy only a second to realise that the woman's life depended on what she could do for her. So she acted accordingly.

A swift examination told her that there was no outward sign of broken bones but she took great care nevertheless as she touched her. The woman was in shock. The pupils of her eyes were dilated and she was breathing with difficulty. The bluish colour in her face immediately aroused Mandy's concern. She gently placed her fingers against the injured woman's face and knew before she did so that the skin would be cold and clammy.

Mandy took off her own jacket and was placing it under the woman's feet when a man's voice inquired gruffly: "Do you need any help nurse?"

Mandy nodded, thinking that his face was vaguely familiar.

He smiled. "I'm a porter at St Adrian's. You are Nurse Greenwood?"

"Yes. We need an ambulance and a policeman. I can't leave her."

"Don't worry. I will see to it!" he exclaimed as he hurried off to the nearest telephone booth.

Meanwhile the woman had opened her eyes. She looked dazed at first then very frightened.

"What has happened?" she whispered in a strained voice.

Mandy swiftly calmed her panic. "You have had a slight accident," she explained quietly. Reassuringly she went on, "You will be all right. Hold my hand . . . no, don't try to move. You have to lie flat until a doctor examines you."

"How do you know?" the woman muttered.

Mandy guessed that the woman was unable to see clearly and had not recognised her uniform. "I'm a nurse. It is best that you should lie quietly."

The woman tried to speak. Mandy leaned over to listen and discovered that the victim had suffered a collapse. She was giving her artificial respiration when the ambulance arrived.

Forgetting about the policeman, Mandy climbed in with the patient so that she could give the men the details of what had been happening. By the time they reached the hospital the ambulance men had restored the woman's breathing and were able to remove the oxygen mask.

It was not surprising that after all this Mandy was very late on reaching her ward. Sister had left instructions with the Staff Nurse. Mandy was to be sent to the office immediately!

"This won't do, Greenwood!" Sister Blake said reprimanding her curtly. "You are nearly an hour late! What happened? Did you oversleep? I was told that you were out late last night."

"Yes, I was. But that is not why I am late," Mandy said defensively. "I set off at my usual time. There was a road accident. I stopped to look after the victim."

"I see . . . ! That's a different picture altogether." Sister smiled. "Were you the only one there?"

"Yes. The car didn't stop. I did what I could. It was shock mainly. She's in hospital now."

"That was an excellent experience for you. Did you panic at first? It would be natural in the circumstances."

Mandy shook her head. "I didn't have time. I was too concerned about the woman."

Sister nodded. "I'm sure you did well. Now get back to your duties.

But report to Staff Nurse first."

Later on that morning, Mandy was able to share her coffee break with Audrey who was eager to hear all the details.

"I think all the staff has heard what happened to you," she teased. "You are quite the little heroine! By this evening the incident will be so exaggerated that you will be recommended for a medal."

Mandy laughed. "I didn't do much. I was getting a bit scared that I wouldn't be able to resuscitate her. Luckily the ambulance came in time."

"Was she as bad as that?"

"It was the shock of the accident mainly. I intend to go and see how she is later on."

"Shock can kill. We have been taught that frequently," Audrey said. "It was fortunate that you kept your wits about you."

"Yes." Mandy looked grave. "It's very different when you are alone and confronted by that kind of incident.

The responsibility weighs heavily. But then on the other hand that gives you more confidence."

"I know what you mean."

"She is being kept under observation in one of the side units on the next floor," Mandy told her. "I might not have time this afternoon so I will go now."

"Good idea!" Audrey said. "It will only take a few minutes. I hope you find that she is okay."

Dr Guthrie came from the lift as Mandy was about to enter. He took her by the arm and pulled her aside.

"Take the next one," he said. "Where are you off to?" He broke off and smiled at her startled face. "You needn't tell me! I can guess. You are going to see your patient."

She frowned. "I look after many patients."

"You are prevaricating! You know full well what I mean."

She smiled. "How did you find out?"

"News travels fast in this place. Apparently you came to the rescue just in time."

He looked so attractive with the light from the high windows streaming down on his dark head that Mandy's heart lurched a little. There were tired lines under his eyes. It was almost all she could do to prevent herself from gently touching them with her finger-tips. She was instantly aghast at herself for even thinking of it. Yet she longed to say something more personal . . . more serious. Just a few words with more warmth in them than the casual exchanges that had been presented.

"You are dreamy this morning!" he exclaimed.

There had been such a hostile note in his voice that she glanced at him in surprise. His eyes were showing resentment also.

"Is that a crime?" she asked rather sharply.

"It rather depends on the cause, doesn't it?" he said bluntly.

She smiled secretively. "I can't tell you that."

His thick black eyebrows drew together. "I thought not!" He half turned away then hesitated to add gruffly, "Reggie telephoned me this morning."

"Oh, that was quick! We were talking of you last night," Mandy said without thinking sensibly.

"So I gathered! Reggie was very enthusiastic. He spoke of you in such high terms that I could only assume he was trying to give me a hint as to what might happen. He seemed over the moon. What *did* you promise him?"

Mandy was having difficulty in controlling her anger. It wasn't the words so much as the contempt in which he had uttered them that rankled.

"You have no right to speak to me like that!" she said sharply. "Reggie is an old friend. He gave Audrey and me a grand time. He is a generous and kind-hearted person. Read whatever you like into his remarks but don't accuse me of behaving badly!" Mandy had never been so angry or felt so humiliated. He had practically accused her of disloyalty. Why should he expect that from her when he showed no sign of wanting her affection!

She went on more evenly but still coolly, "I can't see that it is anything to do with you how Audrey and I spend our free time."

At first Leigh had stepped back as if she had struck him. Now he looked very shaken, stricken with remorse. Her response had swiftly brought him to his senses.

"Mandy! You can't believe that I want to upset you? I apologise if I seemed interfering. But it was Reggie's cheek in telephoning me, to tell me he had taken you out, that stuck in my throat. It made me furious!"

"Why should it do that?" Mandy stared at him stubbornly. She was not going to let him off easily. "I'm independent and can make my own decisions."

"I agree. That is why it hurts so much. My hands are tied. You are free to do as you like. That's what frightens me." He thrust his hands into his trouser pockets and turned away.

"Don't go yet!" Her voice sounded very determined. "We ought to clear this up now."

He swung round looking slightly astonished. "I have apologised!" he said curtly. "What else do you want?"

She smiled faintly. "I haven't the time or the inclination to discuss that. It would be wiser not to see each other too often. You become angry every time we meet."

His face whitened. "Don't discard me altogether!" he exclaimed roughly. He grasped her hands and squeezed them so tightly that she winced with pain.

Fortunately the corridor was empty and nobody witnessed the incident. She felt distressed yet annoyed that he was so insensible to her feelings.

"It would be impossible not to encounter each other in the hospital," she told him coolly. "So you needn't worry about being ignored."

He flinched at her indifference. Then his lips twisted wryly.

"Aren't you being rather foolish? It doesn't sound like you at all. Believe me, Mandy, I don't get angry with you! Circumstances are against us, that's all."

"If that is the case why don't you discuss the problem with me?"

"I can't do that. It would involve you," he said flatly.

He looked so stern and stubborn that Mandy stared at him helplessly. She felt bewildered and uncertain and was swiftly losing what little confidence she had left.

She laughed shortly. "You have only confirmed what I was saying. Any relationship between us is impossible. Goodbye, Leigh! No doubt I shall see you around."

He bit his lips in vexation. Then with an air of determination he stalked off with his white coat flapping in protest.

After a swift glance at her fob watch, Mandy decided to return to the ward. She had been due back a few minutes ago and did not want to incur Sister's wrath. While she had been talking to Leigh the time had flown. Tears were stinging her eyes and she had to pause halfway to wipe them away.

The encounter with Leigh had shaken her more than she had realised. Her knees felt like cotton wool and she was on the brink of dissolving into tears.

He is never going to tell me about Irene and her sister, she told herself frustratedly. I was right in my attitude! The situation is ridiculous! Why was he angry because Reggie took me out? Was it jealousy? Or, was it fear of what Reggie might tell me?

It is more likely to have been the latter, she told herself unhappily. If he cared for me he would tell me, wouldn't he? You have to have trust.

He's made it very apparent that he doesn't trust me!

Staff Nurse signalled to her as she entered the ward. Mandy quickly composed herself. She did not want any undue attention.

"A policeman is waiting for you in Sister's office," Moira told her. "It's about that hit and run case."

Mandy nodded. "Is Sister there?"

"Yes. They have been waiting for you so get a move on!"

Mandy was unable to tell the policeman much.

"I did manage to take down the registration number," she said after he had questioned her. "It all happened so fast. I'm afraid I didn't see who was driving the car."

The young policeman smiled. "You did pretty well! Now, nurse, if you could let me have that number I won't keep you any longer."

Mandy glanced nervously at Sister. "I jotted it down in my notebook and I left it in my locker."

Sister frowned. "It's nearly lunch time. You can leave now and take it to the police station."

"No need for that, Sister," the policeman said cheerfully. "I will wait for her. It will be quicker that way."

"Very well, constable!" Sister said sharply. "Nurse! I shall expect you back at your usual time."

It was a rush to find something to eat then return to the hospital on time. Mrs Torrance would have helped if she had been in but unfortunately she had gone out for the day.

"You missed a super lunch today," Audrey informed her when they joined forces that afternoon.

Mandy sighed as she watched Audrey prepare Sister's tea. She wanted it earlier than usual because one of the consultants was coming in to see her.

"Don't rub it in! I had an awful morning."

Audrey grinned. "I know. If you don't hurry up with that bread and butter you will be in more trouble!"

Then relenting a little she went on, "I have some good news for you. Sister is going away for a few days. I overheard her talking to Sister Foster."

Mandy looked interested. "Really? Did she say where she was going?"

"Yes. I felt rather guilty at the time. I was stuck behind a door in one of the units. I had just been to see Marie but I didn't want Sister to know. She might have sent me somewhere before my lunch break. You know what the canteen is like later! Unfortunately I was unable to move and was forced to listen to the conversation, praying all the time that they wouldn't discover me!"

Mandy chuckled. "It would have been very embarrassing."

"You're telling me! More so because Irene sounded so upset. I didn't know she had a sister."

"Frances . . . She's in a mental home."

"That throws some light on what she said!" Audrey was looking more confident. "Apparently, Sister's mother has been taken ill. She lives up north somewhere and has nobody to look after her. Irene has asked for compassionate leave but is worried about her sister. She always tries to visit her on Sundays. As far as I could gather, she was hoping that Foster would offer to go."

"She wasn't too keen about that. Am I right?" Mandy said.

"She said rather hurriedly that she would be too busy. She advised Irene to ask one of the nurses."

Mandy glanced at her friend thoughtfully. "I will go for her. I haven't planned anything for Sunday."

"You would be taking an awful risk!" Audrey exclaimed looking surprised.

"I doubt whether she is very disturbed. Anyway, it would make no difference. I would go if Irene asked me."

"Rather you than me! Okay, I will drop a hint or two." Audrey glanced at her fob watch and sighed. "Another two hours yet! It does seem a long day."

Mandy nodded. "We seem to be rather unsettled lately. The two men going off like that didn't help."

"Oh, I didn't tell you!" Audrey exclaimed. "I had a letter from Leslie. It is definite. They aren't coming back. He asked me to thank you and Mrs Torrance. He and Vivien are going to finish their vacation with friends in Scotland."

"How disappointing!"

"I felt very sad when I started to read the letter. But he did add a postscript. He wants me to write to him and said that perhaps we could meet again in his country. He suggests I take my holiday there." Audrey's eyes filled with tears. "I was absolutely shattered! I never imagined he cared, too."

Mandy gave her a quick hug and kissed her cheek. "You deserve all the happiness you can get. I was hoping something like that would happen. I bet they had made some arrangement between them."

214

"Leslie did say once that Vivien had a girl back home."

"I expect neither of them wanted to get involved. Leslie wants to get to know you before he commits himself."

Audrey nodded. "I realise that now and it's made me so happy. I shall look forward to writing to him."

Staff Nurse opened the door and stared at them suspiciously. "What are you two up to now? Sister will be in any moment and the patients are asking for their tea. You can't expect the juniors to do everything! I don't want to report you to Sister. It's not a good day for that!"

"So she has noticed, too!" Audrey muttered. "Gosh! Is that the time? I forgot we are supervising the teas today."

★ ★ ★

Sister detained Mandy as she was leaving on Friday evening. Audrey gave her friend a reassuring glance as she passed and Mandy's feeling of dismay disappeared. She had forgotten about Audrey's promise. Now she guessed that she had been successful in dropping her hint.

There was no doubt that Sister appeared harassed. She looked tired and much older. Mandy instantly felt sorry for her. I wouldn't want to hurt her, she thought. She has always treated us fairly.

"Don't look so serious!" Sister exclaimed brightly making the effort to change her mood. "I'm not going to reprimand you. I want you to do me a favour."

Mandy looked suitably surprised. "Yes, of course, if I can," she replied.

Sister had turned to gaze out of the window so Mandy was unable to see her face. The woman seemed uneasy as she explained jerkily.

"I have to go away for a few days. Unfortunately I promised my sister, Frances, that I would visit her on Sunday."

"Wouldn't she understand if you told her?"

Sister swung round and stared at her uncertainly. "No, I'm afraid she wouldn't take it in. That's it, you see! I feel very anxious. She had a mental breakdown some time ago. She has improved but she becomes upset very quickly. It wouldn't do for me to tell her that I can't come."

"I see. No wonder you are worried!"

"I don't want to disappoint her. She has so few visitors."

Mandy said diffidently, "Perhaps I could take your place."

Irene gave a sigh of relief. "I would be so thankful if you would. She is more your age than mine. I'm sure you will become friends right away. Also because you are a nurse you will ignore any strangeness in her manner."

"Would she like some flowers or something to eat?" Mandy asked.

Sister smiled gratefully. "That is kind of you! But I don't expect you to pay for them. I will give you the money for the flowers if you wouldn't mind buying them. She gets enough to eat."

"Where do I have to go?"

"I will write it down for you. Don't mention my name unless she asks you where I am."

Mandy looked at her inquiringly. "What do I say to that?"

Sister frowned. "It's difficult to think of a suitable explanation. I don't want to tell her that mother is ill."

"I could say that you have to work and that you will call in later in the week," Mandy said tentatively.

"Yes." Sister smiled and brightened up considerably. "I ought to be back in a few days. It is good of you, Mandy! I know your spare time is precious."

Mandy was reading the writing on the piece of paper she had been given. "Richmond! One of my favourite places! I shall enjoy going there," she remarked.

"There is one stipulation," Irene told her. She looked slightly embarrassed. "I would rather you went on your own and kept this to yourself."

Mandy nodded. "I understand. That's no problem. I'm the only one in my group with time off on Sunday. I needn't mention exactly where I'm going. Lots of people visit Richmond Park. But I don't suppose any of them will be interested enough to ask me."

8

SUNDAY, surprisingly enough, turned out to be a warm sunny day. There had been downpours in the week and Mandy had resigned herself for a long damp walk wearing boots and a raincoat.

But when she saw the sunshine, she settled for a pale green summer dress and white sandals. It was a treat to have an occasion to dress up for. Her attire would be so different to her usual uniform and sensible shoes.

Feeling very presentable, she set off. But the nervous feeling that she had ignored in the excitement of getting away for a few hours, returned with increasing force as she neared her destination.

The waterside nursing home was situated a mile outside the town. As it was well known, Mandy had no difficulty in finding it. The place looked very grand with its tree-lined walk, vast lawns and flower beds.

Mandy had purchased some flowers from a stall near the station and supplemented them with a gift of candy from herself. The drive to the entrance seemed endless. By the time she reached the open doors she was breathless as well as being extremely apprehensive.

Supposing Frances took a dislike to her? Would she react violently? Would she be angry because her sister couldn't come?

Luckily Mandy did not have long to dwell on her misgivings. The desk clerk greeted her pleasantly and asked her to sit down whilst inquiries were made. A few minutes later, a nurse in a pale pink uniform with a tiny cap on her neat head, arrived. She went over to Mandy.

"You are Nurse Greenwood? Come with me! We have been expecting you. Sister Blake informed us yesterday."

Mandy smiled faintly. "I'm pleased she did that. I was doubtful about being allowed to visit Frances."

"She loves having visitors. At the moment she is helping in the playroom. If you wish I will take you there."

"Do you have children here as well?" Mandy asked.

"Too many, unfortunately. We are glad of any help we can get."

"Are they all mentally disturbed?" Mandy asked as she followed her into the lift.

The nurse looked at her in surprise. "We are not a mental home!"

"Forgive me! I was told Frances was mentally ill so naturally I assumed the other patients were also."

"We do have one or two patients who are mentally disturbed. Frances is well on the way to recovery now. She is a lively person and very popular with us all."

By now Mandy was unsure of what to expect; certainly not the lovely young person she saw in the midst of a group of child patients. They were clamouring for her attention. Mandy's first impression was of a mass of dark hair above huge brown eyes. When the nurse called out to Frances and the girl stood up, Mandy gained a clearer view of her. She looked slimmer and younger than her twenty or so years. And there was an undeniable resemblance to Irene.

Expecting somebody unbalanced and perhaps unreasonable, Mandy was agreeably surprised with the reception she received. The nurse who had escorted her to the playroom left them after she had taken them to a private unit where they would be able to converse in peace.

"Do you work in the same hospital as my sister?" Frances inquired with interest after they had sat down.

"Yes. I work under her. I'm one of her nurses," Mandy told her with a friendly smile.

"Really? What is she like? Is she bossy?"

Mandy chuckled. "All Sisters are sometimes. Your sister is well liked."

"That's good." Frances dropped the subject as if bored with it and went off at a tangent. It was then that Mandy began to doubt if the girl was as balanced as she seemed at first.

"Have you met Derek Forester yet?" Frances asked eagerly. "He is one of the doctors here. He's promised to take me to a theatre when I'm quite well. I can't wait although he keeps telling me to be patient."

Mandy said understandingly, "I'm sure that day won't be far off. You look very well."

Frances frowned. "It's not my health that is keeping me here." The girl leaned forward and whispered secretively, "They wouldn't tell you why they won't let me go. You see they need help so badly they couldn't allow me to leave. They know I'm fully recovered but they pretend otherwise. I'm too useful to them. Can you understand that?"

"Yes, naturally you couldn't let them

down!" Mandy replied hastily, stifling her uneasiness.

The girl nodded complacently. "Yes. It's very important that I stay for a time. Derek agrees with me. He knows all about *them*. He's such an understanding man."

"I'm sure he is," Mandy said quietly.

There was an exultant lilt in Frances' voice as she went on excitedly, "I'm going to marry him one day. Don't tell anyone! It's a secret."

The girl looked so vulnerable and lovely as she seriously affirmed her intention that Mandy drew in a painful breath. What could she say? She was overwhelmed with pity for the unfortunate young woman. Yet she seemed happy enough. There had been no mention of Leigh. Mandy doubted if Frances even remembered him!

The sweets were received more enthusiastically than the flowers. Mandy's assumption that they might be more of a luxury had been correct. Hospitals usually had plenty of flowers.

"Will you come again?" she was asked eagerly.

"I expect so," Mandy said. "I wasn't going to leave just yet."

The girl's face lit up. "I'm used to Irene. She's always in a hurry and gets cross with me. I never get time to tell her about Derek. She won't listen. She is going to be surprised one day!"

"I think she will be," Mandy said. "Is Derek more important to you than anyone else?"

Frances gave her an indignant stare. "That's a stupid question! I told you we are going to be married."

"So you did. It was silly of me." Mandy paused then smiled. "Tell me what you do here most days."

"I look after the children. That's my job." Frances smiled maliciously. "My sister isn't the only one who can run a ward!"

"I'm sure you do it very well. The kiddies seemed very fond of you."

"They are easy to deal with. Adults

are more of a problem. They interfere and want me to do as they say." Frances stared at her earnestly. "That doesn't mean you. I like you, Mandy. You don't criticise or argue. You will come again?"

"I will come if I'm allowed to."

"They can't stop you! This isn't a prison," the girl said belligerently.

Mandy hastened to talk of other things. "What do you prefer to do each day?" she asked pleasantly.

Frances smiled. "I try to go out to look around. The grounds are so big and pretty."

Mandy stayed another thirty minutes. Frances was enjoying her company so much that Mandy would have stayed longer. But the nurse who had introduced them came to warn her that visiting time was up.

The last thing Mandy could remember was the lost, rather bewildered expression on the lovely face of Irene's unfortunate sister. All the way out of the building, the tears threatened to overflow. But when she reached the sunlit driveway she could no longer hold them back. She was alone with her grief or so she thought. A car passed her, slowing down as it approached the main entrance. Mandy scarcely noticed it as she stemmed the stream of tears with her handkerchief.

"Mandy!"

It was a very loud, astonished cry and it brought Mandy to an abrupt halt. She turned and saw Leigh getting out of his car a few yards back. He walked swiftly towards her.

"What on earth are you doing here?" he demanded rather sternly. "I couldn't believe my eyes when I passed you just now." His eyes narrowed as he scrutinised her wan face. "You have been crying! What's the matter?"

Subtlety forgotten, Mandy blurted out, "I've been to visit Frances."

Leigh stared at her blankly. "Why? How do you know her?" he demanded.

Mandy shook her head. "I saw her today for the first time. Sister Blake was unable to come. She asked me to stand in for her."

Leigh laughed hollowly. "After all the trouble I've taken to keep you apart, she did this to you!" He sounded frustrated and unhappy.

"What is so terrible about seeing Frances?" Mandy asked.

"She upset you, didn't she?" he said gravely.

"It wasn't her fault. My stupid feelings got the better of me," Mandy replied defensively.

Leigh tilted her tear stained face so that he could kiss the unhappiness from her soft lips. "Oh, Mandy, I do love you! You are such a sweet person. I wish I could have spared you this."

"Don't make a tragedy out of it!" she said with a faint smile. "It was only a visit to a nursing home. I see people in the same condition every day."

She was feeling slightly bewildered wondering whether his declaration was serious or merely an exaggerated expression to make her feel he was disturbed by her being there. If his previous behaviour was anything to go by it was meaningless.

Leigh sighed. "I feel very angry. Irene has a lot to answer for!"

"Why do you say that?" Mandy eyed him curiously. "Why are you here today?"

"That's a good question! I shall have to explain now." Leigh glanced around him. "It's very exposed here. Shall we stroll through the woods?"

"Were you on your way to visit Frances?" Mandy asked.

Leigh looked surprised. "I suppose Irene has told you!" he exclaimed bitterly.

Mandy shook her head. "I've only gleaned scraps from the grape-vine. None of it makes sense."

"I'm not surprised! It's a confusing situation. I hardly know where to start," Leigh told her ruefully.

"At the beginning would be best," Mandy said practically. "Did you meet Irene or Frances first?"

"I worked with Sister Blake during my two years stint as a senior house officer. Then I extended the field a little and became a locum."

"That is when you met Frances," Mandy stated.

Leigh smiled wryly. "You do know a lot! She was one of the patients I had to treat. Unfortunately, as it happened, I was never the same individual afterwards."

"How could she have affected you that much? Did you fall in love with her?"

"No! She destroyed my peace of mind. Like you, I was deeply moved. I became terribly concerned about her mental state. But that was after I had finished as a locum."

"Why didn't you just leave all the worry behind? Doctors and nurses can't become involved with their patients."

Leigh smiled crookedly. "I was ready to do that but Irene had different ideas."

Mandy took his hand. "Please go on!

I will understand."

"Bless you!" Leigh's hand stole across her shoulders and drew her closer to him. "It will be good to talk about it. Irene and her sister lived in a big house in Chiswick. I made a fatal mistake when I accepted an invitation to go there for a meal. I had already sensed that Frances was viewing me more intimately than I could allow. She was a beautiful girl but at that time I had a girl friend. To make things worse it became obvious after a period of time that Irene was encouraging her sister. Eventually it came to a head one evening when Irene deliberately left Frances and me alone and the girl declared that she intended to marry me."

"How did you deal with that?" Mandy asked curiously.

He laughed shortly. "Very foolishly! I'm afraid I was much too blunt. I told her I had no intention of marrying her because I was engaged to another girl."

"Sister Mortimer," Mandy said softly.

Leigh groaned. "You have heard about her, too!"

"Only that she left to go abroad and that it was because of you."

"Irene did that! I never found out what method or words she used. Anita refused to see me and sent back my ring. She didn't give me a chance to explain." Leigh's glance was filled with anguish. "That's why I was so frightened when I fell in love with you. I couldn't declare myself. If Irene had found out she would have ruined any relationship between us."

Mandy's lovely eyes misted with tears of joy. "You do care for me! If only you had said something . . . anything at all . . . to give me some hope. I believed it was all on my side. I was giving up . . . pretending to myself that I didn't care."

Leigh swept her into his arms and kissed her as if he never intended to let her go. At last he muttered gruffly: "I care for you, Mandy. Don't ever doubt that again! I was terrified of losing you. I had to fool the world that I wasn't interested. Irene watched me constantly and never allowed me to forget where my allegiance lay. I felt hopelessly trapped . . . tied to her irretrievably."

"What did she expect you to do?"

Leigh smiled twistedly. "Marry her sister! There was no doubt about that. It was mentioned every time she approached me. If only I could have been wise before the event I would not have spoken out as I did. There had been no mention of the girl's mental state in the doctor's file. It was only afterwards when Frances had the breakdown that I fully understood how instrumental I had been in her collapse." He smiled grimly. "That fact Irene has never allowed me to forget."

"I understand now why you had those quarrels," Mandy said pensively.

"What could you know about those?"

"I saw you and Irene in the Lamb

one evening. She struck you."

"Oh, no!" Leigh's face had whitened. "The humiliation is too much. It's fortunate that I knew nothing of your presence there. I might have done her some injury. I felt cheapened and angry enough as it was."

Mandy pressed her head against his shoulder. "It's all over now."

"Is it?" he asked bitterly. "When Irene learns of our attachment it won't be long before she tries to alienate you."

"It won't work this time because I have met Frances and I know all the facts." Mandy smiled up at him. "I believe your worries are over. Frances isn't in love with you any more. Dr Derek Forester is the apple of her eye at the moment. She talked constantly of him. He is the one she intends to marry. She told me so."

"Forester?" Leigh looked surprised. "I was at medical school with him. Poor fool! It's a pretty grim outlook for him."

"He won't make the same mistake you did. He is aware of her history." Mandy slid her hand into his and moved back so that she could see him more clearly. "Irene is the one to be pitied," she said soberly. "Frances is happy with her games of pretence. The nurse said she is nearly well. How can that be?"

"She will appear normal. She might never have another breakdown. I would have to be the person to trigger one off!"

"What made you come here today? Were you going to see Frances?"

"No! That would have been sheer lunacy! I knew Irene was away. She had been nagging at me so much I thought I would come here and make my own inquiries. She was beginning to get under my skin. I was actually starting to feel guilty."

Mandy sighed. "Irene is such a sensible nurse. Why couldn't she realise her sister wasn't normal?"

"She believed her mental state was

due to disappointment over me. That's why she wants us to marry. According to her everything revolves round that. Irene is convinced that if her sister achieves her ambition it will keep her sane."

Mandy frowned. "She doesn't show much concern for you! Supposing it didn't work?"

"Irene is oblivious to my feelings." He smiled wryly. "Frances has to be kept happy at all costs."

"Let's forget Irene and Frances," Mandy said quietly. "It's such a lovely afternoon. The air smells so good under the trees. Do you have to rush off anywhere?"

"No. I'm free until eleven o'clock." Leigh laughed and kissed her swiftly. "It's time I did that more convincingly. Will you marry me, Mandy? Soon I mean. No long engagements this time!"

Mandy's green eyes teased. "You will have to explain Sister Mortimer to me first!" she told him lightly.

He shrugged his broad shoulders. "It was a mistake. If she had been serious about me, she would have ignored Irene and come to me for an explanation."

Mandy glanced at him curiously. "What about you? Were you upset?"

"I was angry. Later on I felt reprieved."

She said gravely, "Perhaps Irene did you a good turn after all."

"Yes. It might have been difficult after I met you." Leigh's grey eyes were tenderly caressing. "Darling Mandy . . . ! It hasn't been easy for you. I will make it up to you. Loving you has been the best thing that has ever happened to me."

She laughed happily. "Why that's exactly how I've been feeling about you!" she exclaimed.

Time slipped by unnoticed as she returned to his loving arms.

WITH SOMEBODY ELSE
Theresa Charles

Rosamond sets off for Cornwall with Hugo to meet his family, blissfully unaware of the shocks in store for her.

A SUMMER FOR STRANGERS
Claire Hamilton

Because she had lost her job, her flat and she had no money, Tabitha agreed to pose as Adam's future wife although she believed the scheme to be deceitful and cruel.

VILLA OF SINGING WATER
Angela Petron

The disquieting incidents that occurred at the Vatican and the Colosseum did not trouble Jan at first, but then they became increasingly unpleasant and alarming.

DOCTOR NAPIER'S NURSE
Pauline Ash

When cousins Midge and Derry are entered as probationer nurses on the same day but at different hospitals they agree to exchange identities.

A GIRL LIKE JULIE
Louise Ellis

Caroline absolutely adored Hugh Barrington, but then Julie Crane came into their lives. Julie was the kind of girl who attracts men without even trying.

COUNTRY DOCTOR
Paula Lindsay

When Evan Richmond bought a practice in a remote country village he did not realise that a casual encounter would lead to the loss of his heart.

ENCORE
Helga Moray

Craig and Janet realise that their true happiness lies with each other, but it is only under traumatic circumstances that they can be reunited.

NICOLETTE
Ivy Preston

When Grant Alston came back into her life, Nicolette was faced with a dilemma. Should she follow the path of duty or the path of love?

THE GOLDEN PUMA
Margaret Way

Catherine's time was spent looking after her father's Queensland farm. But what life was there without David, who wasn't interested in her?

HOSPITAL BY THE LAKE
Anne Durham

Nurse Marguerite Ingleby was always ready to become personally involved with her patients, to the despair of Brian Field, the Senior Surgical Registrar, who loved her.

VALLEY OF CONFLICT
David Farrell

Isolated in a hostel in the French Alps, Ann Russell sees her fiancé being seduced by a young girl. Then comes the avalanche that imperils their lives.

NURSE'S CHOICE
Peggy Gaddis

A proposal of marriage from the incredibly handsome and wealthy Reagan was enough to upset any girl — and Brooke Martin was no exception.

A DANGEROUS MAN
Anne Goring

Photographer Polly Burton was on safari in Mombasa when she met enigmatic Leon Hammond. But unpredictability was the name of the game where Leon was concerned.

PRECIOUS INHERITANCE
Joan Moules

Karen's new life working for an authoress took her from Sussex to a foreign airstrip and a kidnapping; to a real life adventure as gripping as any in the books she typed.

VISION OF LOVE
Grace Richmond

When Kathy takes over the rundown country kennels she finds Alec Stinton, a local vet, very helpful. But their friendship arouses bitter jealousy and a tragedy seems inevitable.

CRUSADING NURSE
Jane Converse

It was handsome Dr. Corbett who opened Nurse Susan Leighton's eyes and who set her off on a lonely crusade against some powerful enemies and a shattering struggle against the man she loved.

WILD ENCHANTMENT
Christina Green

Rowan's agreeable new boss had a dream of creating a famous perfume using her precious Silverstar, but Rowan's plans were very different.

DESERT ROMANCE
Irene Ord

Sally agrees to take her sister Pam's place as La Chartreuse the dancer, but she finds out there is more to it than dyeing her hair red and looking like her sister.

HEART OF ICE
Marie Sidney

How was January to know that not only would the warmth of the Swiss people thaw out her frozen heart, but that she too would play her part in helping someone to live again?

LUCKY IN LOVE
Margaret Wood

Companion-secretary to wealthy gambler Laura Duxford, who lived in Monaco, seemed to Melanie a fabulous job. Especially as Melanie had already lost her heart to Laura's son, Julian.

NURSE TO PRINCESS JASMINE
Lilian Woodward

Nick's surgeon brother, Tom, performs an operation on an Arabian princess, and she invites Tom, Nick and his fiancé to Omander, where a web of deceit and intrigue closes about them.

THE WAYWARD HEART
Eileen Barry

Disaster-prone Katherine's nickname was "Kate Calamity", but her boss went too far with an outrageous proposal, which because of her latest disaster, she could not refuse.

FOUR WEEKS IN WINTER
Jane Donnelly

Tessa wasn't looking forward to meeting Paul Mellor again — she had made a fool of herself over him once before. But was Orme Jared's solution to her problem likely to be the right one?

SURGERY BY THE SEA
Sheila Douglas

Medical student Meg hadn't really wanted to go and work with a G.P. on the Welsh coast although the job had its compensations. But Owen Roberts was certainly not one of them!

HEAVEN IS HIGH
Anne Hampson

The new heir to the Manor of Marbeck had been found. But it was rather unfortunate that when he arrived unexpectedly he found an uninvited guest, complete with stetson and high boots.

LOVE WILL COME
Sarah Devon

June Baker's boss was not really her idea of her ideal man, but when she went from third typist to boss's secretary overnight she began to change her mind.

ESCAPE TO ROMANCE
Kay Winchester

Oliver and Jean first met on Swale Island. They were both trying to begin their lives afresh, but neither had bargained for complications from the past.

CASTLE IN THE SUN
Cora Mayne

Emma's invalid sister, Kym, needed a warm climate, and Emma jumped at the chance of a job on a Mediterranean island. But Emma soon finds that intrigues and hazards lurk on the sunlit isle.

BEWARE OF LOVE
Kay Winchester

Carol Brampton resumes her nursing career when her family is killed in a car accident. With Dr. Patrick Farrell she begins to pick up the pieces of her life, but is bitterly hurt when insinuations are made about her to Patrick.

DARLING REBEL
Sarah Devon

When Jason Farradale's secretary met with an accident, her glamorous stand-in was quite unable to deal with one problem in particular.

THE PRICE OF PARADISE
Jane Arbor

It was a shock to Fern to meet her estranged husband on an island in the middle of the Indian Ocean, but to discover that her father had engineered it puzzled Fern. What did he hope to achieve?

DOCTOR IN PLASTER
Lisa Cooper

When Dr. Scott Sutcliffe is injured, Nurse Caroline Hurst has to cope with a very demanding private case. But when she realises her exasperating patient has stolen her heart, how can Caroline possibly stay?

A TOUCH OF HONEY
Lucy Gillen

Before she took the job as secretary to author Robert Dean, Cadie had heard how charming he was, but that wasn't her first impression at all.